Heartstrings

By Heather Gunter

This book is dedicated to all of the strong women
and men who have endured and survived rape.
Who realize
that they were never a victim but always a survivor.

Bruised, Battered and Broken

I was bruised that night, not because you yanked and pulled on me, but because you hurt me emotionally.

I was battered that night, not because you hit and bit me but because you made me feel like I was less of a person.

I was broken that night, not because you physically broke a bone, but because you took something that didn't belong to you.

I will no longer feel bruised, battered and broken, I refuse to give you that power, because I have taken it back.

Written by Heather Gunter
at 19 yrs of age

Contents

Prologue

It's spring break here in Georgia, and we all decided to spend the day at the lake. It looks like we might be heading into an early summer. The weather in Georgia is unpredictable most of the time; one day cool, the next hot and humid.

It's just the four of us. Will, Maverick, Charlie, and Me. Yes, Maverick and Charlie have made their way back to each other; they're stuck to each other like glue. I don't think he'll ever make the mistake he did last time. Maverick's knee is healed, but he still fights a slight limp. He'll never play professional football, but seems content with it. As smart as he is, he'll probably end up with an academic scholarship and try his hand at something else.

Charlie's come a long way. She's finally happy. Happier than I have ever seen her, but she still has moments of insecurity. I think she always will. Charlie finally sees what we have seen all along; she's an awesome, beautiful girl and a great friend. There's nothing ordinary about Charlie. She faced the problem when she was ready, and now she holds her head up and smiles all of the time. Maverick is usually making her laugh, or my smartass mouth.

The very first time I met my friend, she was just a shell of the person she is now. She was broken and beaten and I knew I needed to be her friend. Sometimes you can just sense someone needs you, and I sensed that about her. But what she never realized is I needed her just as much.

Her parents still won't speak to her and I think it bothers her, in a small way. She still lives with my mom and me, and she's become a permanent part of my family. We even irritate each other like sisters.

And then there's Will, who refuses to find a girl, no matter how many times I have told him to, and it's a little awkward when the four of us are together, and I tend to be the 'mouthy' red-head Will likes to call me. And yeah, I can also be a complete bitch at times. I think Charlie and Maverick expect Will and I to eventually get together, but it's not that easy. It will never be that easy. Will is a great guy, but we went down this road before and we can't do it again. Sure, he's hot as hell with his blond-streaked hair and green eyes, tall with a muscular swimmers frame. I'm attracted to him; I would be crazy not to be. I won't deny there are sparks because there are, but some things can never be.

You see, despite the "all put together" persona I show the world, I have my own insecurities and have things I just can't talk about. We all have our own secrets. Mine is a doozy, and I am completely ashamed of it.

I sit here on this beautiful spring day and realize what a hypocrite I am. Charlie faced her fears and talked to her parents, but I refuse to share anything about my secret. I really don't mean to be hypocritical, but I have to figure things out on my own. Even if it means being alone.

Damaged Goods

Chapter 1

Tori

My senses begin to take over and I leave my eyes closed; I don't want to see. It's always the same bits and pieces all over again and I never open my eyes. I use my senses to just listen, smell and feel.

I feel cold, and pressure—lots and lots of pressure. My legs are stuck. Stuck against what I assume to be some kind of vinyl. The skin on my legs is sticking against it. It hurts to move. When I attempt to pull my legs away, even just a little bit, there's no relief. I'm pressed as far into it as I can possibly get. I don't doubt my body has created an indention in it. I'm scared. Then, I realize why I can't move my legs: they're being held down by something. My hands are above my head, being held by what feels like skin.

All of a sudden I hear a laugh. A hate filled laugh that resonates throughout my bones, and it shakes me to my very core. I've heard this laugh before, but I can't place it. I just know that I've heard it and it terrifies me.

I take a deep breath, trying to calm myself, but what I smell sends my stomach into a revolt. Alcohol and cigarette breath that reeks and makes me want to heave. I begin to panic when I hear that laugh again as the pressure tightens on my wrists.

Willing, with all my strength, my eyes finally open.

As I open my eyes in a panic, I realize I'm in the safety of my own bed at home. I look around and see everything familiar to me and will myself to slow my breathing down. Not to mention it feels like my heart is going to beat right out of my chest.

"*I'm fine,*" I say out loud. As if saying it out loud will make me believe it. I say this over and over.

I feel a drip of something drizzle down the side of my face. Brushing my cheek with my hand I realize I'm sweating profusely and that I'm soaking wet. I take the top of my sheet and wipe my face. Sighing, I realize clean sheets are now needed. Gross.

My dreams are always bits and pieces of my nightmare. Like every morning, I push them back and try to forget. That's what I do, because I don't want to feel. Feeling causes pain and heartache and I can't handle that, so it's just better to push it away.

I finally sit up and throw the covers off of me. "Shit, it's cold," I exclaim out loud. It may be spring, but damn the mornings are still a bit nippy. I tip toe out of my room and walk into the bathroom. I look at myself in the mirror, noting the bed head. I turn on the faucet and splash some cold water on my face, hoping that it will make the circles around my eyes appear not quite so dark; as if the water is somehow magical. I dry my face with a towel and look again. Nope, it's still there. I'm beginning to resemble a raccoon.

The dreams are starting to get worse and my body shudders, recalling a flash of bits and pieces of the one from this morning. I try desperately to push this all away to the very depths of my mind, hoping that, just maybe, if I bury it deep enough it'll all eventually go away.

"Hey sleepy head, you're up already?"

I jump, startled and turn around quickly. I'm sure I just resembled a girl that had her hand in the cookie jar. "Shit Charlie, you can't sneak up on me like that," I snap.

She flinches at my tone, "I'm sorry, I didn't mean to."

I let out a sigh, feeling like a bitch for snapping. "No, I'm sorry, I didn't mean to snap, you just scared the crap out of me, and I haven't been sleeping very well."

She looks at me with concern, "Anything you want to talk about? You know I'm always here for you."

I start to make my way back to my room, wanting to avoid this conversation. "Nope, I'm good. Thanks for asking. I think I'm just excited and ready to graduate, ya know?"

Yeah, it's a lame answer, I know. But hopefully, it will pacify her.

She follows me to my doorway and sighs, which is a 'Charlie' sign that says she knows I'm full of shit. But I know her well enough to know that she won't push me. She never does and that's one of the things I love about her. She turns around and makes her way across the hall, back to her room.

I feel like such a heel. I know she'd be there for me if I needed her too, she always is. But I know I won't be able to handle the look in her eye, if I was to tell her. I can't bear it. I prefer for her to see me as the happy and carefree girl that she thinks me to be. It's easier that way.

Right?

This morning is decidedly beginning to suck ass already, and I need to try and attempt to shake off this current funk; bad dreams be damned.

I start to feel this instant need to make it up to Charlie for being such a bitch so damn early and I know just how to do it. I cross the hall over to her room and lean against the door frame. She's sitting on her bed cross legged, leaning against the back of her headboard and chewing on her thumbnail, in deep concentration.

"Hey, how about when it warms up this afternoon we go back to the lake?" I start wagging my eyebrows as I say, "Call Maverick, and we'll pack a picnic lunch, and go to your most favorite spot that you two finally decided to share with us special people."

Her head pops up as she instantly brightens and then notices my eyebrows and begins to finally smile. "On one condition," she says.

Well shit, I should have known that it was going to come with a 'condition'.

"What?" I tentatively say, knowing that this can't ever be good. Charlie's conditions almost always come with a small price.

"How about we call Will and see if he wants to come?"

Yep, I was right; I knew this so called condition would entail something that I wouldn't like. But I owe her after my bitchy attitude this morning. Truth be told, Charlie saying Will's name causes my heart to beat in overdrive, which gives me mixed feelings. I decide to play her game and I straighten my shoulders ready to take on her challenge.

"Sure, have Maverick," as I call out in a singsong voice, "Call Will."

She ignores that suggestion and instead says, "Hey T, you wear that bright emerald green two piece you bought last week. You look hot in it and your hair and eyes pop in that color."

Does she think I don't know what she's doing? I'm not an idiot, but for her I'll do it, if it makes up for my earlier behavior. Two can play at this game.

"You know the bikini you bought last week, you know the same day I bought mine?" I say this with just a hint of sarcasm. "I say you brave up and wear it finally." Ha, take that I say to myself.

It's a deep purple that makes her eyes instantly stand out and pop. She looked great in it and I know Maverick would have a flipping conniption fit to see her in it; but in a good way.

Her eyes grow big as saucers at my suggestion, but then I notice a look of determination cross her face. "Fine, I'll wear it."

Hmm, challenge accepted huh? I wasn't expecting that.

This last part I know she's not going to like, "One other thing Char, no cover-up." She begins to bristle and sputter with the last part of my deal. "Nope, you're not backing down. It's time you realize how fantastic you look. Just you wait until Maverick sees you in it."

She holds her chin up higher and I can tell I've won this round, or so I think. "Fine, I'll wear it, but I have another condition of my own. You have to call Will and invite him." Okay, now she's crossed a line that she doesn't realize she's crossed. I start to speak when she holds her hand to shush me.

"You want me to wear the bikini with no cover-up, which you know is a huge deal for me, then you have to do something bigger, call Will yourself."

I blow air out of my mouth I didn't realize I'd been holding.

Well damn her.

"Fine, I'll do it. No big deal." The smile on her face is priceless. It's the same look the Cheshire cat wore in Alice in Wonderland. The stinker.

However, I don't hold back on the eye roll I throw her and hope she notices. Yeah, she does, because she smiles even bigger before I turn around to head into my room. Before I shut my door I hear, "Tori, I love you," in a sing-song voice. She so loves irritating me.

I run my hands through my hair like a freaking idiot.

"He can't see you, you big dope. So why are you worrying about your hair?" I chastise myself. Okay, this won't be hard. I can do this. I am freaking Tori. I'm not scared of anything.

I know full well that's a damn lie. The dreams I'm having say different. Giving myself a mental slap*: I got this, I talk to him all the time, and this is nothing.* Except, a one on one conversation, with no backup, is a completely different story.

Grabbing my phone I take a deep breath and paste on a smile. Psyching myself to believe this really isn't as big of a deal as I'm making it. *But it is…*

One ring, two and then I hear the most masculine voice that literally makes my knees quake, "Hello?" That's all it takes and I'm a big jumble of nerves and can't seem to get any words out of my mouth. "Hello, Tori?" he asks.

Shit! He knows it's me.

Duh! Of course he has my number, I'm such a dumb ass. Knowing I need to finally speak or he's going to think I'm a total nimrod. Finding my voice I spurt out, "Um, hey Will, it's Tori."

Again, I'm such an idiot.

"I was wondering, I mean, we were wondering if you want to come to the lake with me, Charlie and Maverick?" I quickly stammer out.

I hear nothing. Dead silence, except I can still hear him breathing on the line. I know I haven't lost him, but why isn't he speaking?

Freaking A, this is hard.

"Hello, Will?"

I hear a throat clear when he says, "Sorry, Tori, I was just surprised that you would call and invite me."

"Well," I quickly blurt out. "I lost a bet with Charlie and this is my punishment."

"Shit, stupid, stupid."

"I'm sorry Will, I didn't mean it like that," I stammer on... Instead of making me sweat it out he just chuckles and feel instant relief.

"Well, when you ask me like that, how can I refuse? What time, Tori?"

OMG, the way he says my name does things to my insides.

"Um, as soon as it warms up, we're taking a picnic lunch and thought we'd take it to Maverick and Tori's 'secret' place."

"How about I bring the sandwiches and y'all bring everything else?" I close my eyes and just let his southern accent sink into my skin. The way he says "y' all" makes me feel things I have no reason to be feeling. I certainly don't deserve to feel this way.

Finally shaking these strange feelings off and finding my voice I say, "Sounds good Will, noon sound okay?"

"Yep, sounds good, Tori."

"See you there." I say.

"You will. Bye Tori, see you then."

"Okay," I say breathlessly and the phone goes dead.

I lay down on the bed with my phone in my hand and close my eyes. Why is this so hard for me?

Then I remember; *I'm damaged; I'm damaged goods.*

Red is my favorite color

Chapter 2

Will

Talk about a surprise. In no way, shape or form was I ever expecting to hear that voice. It's no shocker to anyone that I have a thing for that 'mouthy' redhead. I can't seem to help myself. Call it self-punishment, I don't care. I don't think I'll ever get over her and I don't think I'll ever want to. I have girls that are interested, but they just don't do 'it' for me.

That red hair of hers is unlike anything you've ever seen or I've ever seen for that matter. There has never been and will never be, a color like hers. I can't even properly begin to describe it. It's the most vibrant of reds. It's like an orangey red, but hell it's not orange. You know the different colors that pass through a flame? It's, it's like looking at the flames of a fire. Amazing!

She is hotness personified. Tori has these green eyes you could lose yourself in; that light up when she's being a smart ass, or when she's laughing. She has a couple a sprinkling of freckles that run right across the bridge of her nose, but she's not fair skinned. She has these long-ass legs that go on for miles that I've fantasized about for far too long. Her voice is something else. She's a singer, like Charlie. Unlike Charlie's crystal clear voice, Tori's voice is raw and husky—the epitome of sexy. It's deep and gravely and, God help me, I'm lost when she sings.

I've been trying to give her space. Hell, a year is a long time to give someone space and I can't seem to do that anymore, and I don't want to. Here we are in our senior year of high school during spring break with only a month and half of school left until we graduate. I can't let things go the way they are; I just need to jump in, head first.

I've never told anyone about Tori and my one and only date. Not even Maverick knows. I love Maverick like a brother, but shit, I don't even know what happened, so how was I going to explain it to him?

Going back to the phone conversation with Tori, I begin to think about the bits and pieces of our short conversation that are just now starting to stick out. If I'm not mistaken, she sounded nervous and a little out of breath. Tori is never nervous, and always on her toes. But she hesitated on the phone.

"Why?"

I may be crazy, but something tells me that she was affected by calling me. My instincts are screaming at me and telling me to pay attention. Even her stating she lost a bet and Charlie made her call me, tells me that this is something I need to remember. The fact Charlie made the bet with Tori having to call me, as the loser, doesn't even bother me. I could kiss Charlie for that, but then I'd have to feel the wrath of Maverick and I'd just as soon not be on his bad side. The thought makes me chuckle, recalling a previous conversation with Maverick when I called Charlie hot. Shit, did I hit a nerve with him, and man was he pissed. He deserved it though, and he needed to get his head out of his ass and stop being so damn stupid. And he did, eventually. Don't get me wrong Charlie's hot, but she's just not the girl for me, and she's certainly no fiery redhead.

But there are things I need to know, like why did she leave me that night and was he worth it? My heart begins to hurt just thinking about that night a year ago. Before that first date we had flirted like crazy, until I'd finally gotten the nerve to ask her out. She said yes instantly, so I thought there was something worth exploring. She looked at me, the way I looked at her—as if time stopped. And when she looked at me, her green eyes would get even greener, which sounds impossible, but they did.

I have so many unanswered questions and I know there has to be more to the story that I'm just not aware of. Tori has never been the same since that night, and she's avoided me like the damn plague for the last year. She won't look me in the eye, or speak to me, unless she has to.

What did I do, to cause her to not speak to me?

I sigh and shake myself out of this funk. I'm a guy and I need to man the hell up and try to get the girl. Because this is a girl I haven't been able to shake myself from, and she is most definitely worth it.

I grab my bathing suit trunks, towel and a cooler and head out to my truck calling Maverick on the way.

He answers on the first ring. "What's up bro? I heard Tori called and invited you to the lake. Are you coming?"

First of all, he knows me well and knows that I'd never miss the chance to spend any time with Tori, so it seems like a dumb question to me. "Um, yeah, Tori lost a bet and didn't get a choice in the matter."

"There's always a choice Will. Do you even for a second believe that Charlie can make her do anything? If she didn't want to call you bro, then she wouldn't have. Simple as that. I know we've never spoken about the 'date', but if you ever need to talk, I'm here dude."

As his words sink in completely, I realize he's right. Tori is strong willed, and if she didn't want to call, then she wouldn't have. If there ever were moments of second guessing myself, they are now dead and buried. I like this fiery girl a lot. And if I'm not mistaken, she likes me back.

I'm a head cocker

Chapter 3

Tori

I hear a tapping on the door and suddenly I see Charlie's head peek around, only showing her face. "Well, did you call him and is he coming?" She asks. There's a hint of excitement in her voice that I can see she's trying hard not show on her face and she's failing. I inwardly chuckle.

"Yes Char, I did. He's meeting us at noon. Do you have the bathing suit on?" I see her face get her typical pink flush when she's either embarrassed or nervous. "I've seen you in it already, so what are you worried about? You know I wouldn't say it looked good on you if it didn't. You know I'm as honest as it comes."

I am such a liar. I feel a twinge of guilt start to seep through and then quickly tell myself, *"When it comes to Charlie, and helping her feel better about herself, I am always honest."*

She gingerly opens the door all the way and stands in the doorway. The deep purple is a perfect color for her. The suit is a halter style that wraps around her neck. It makes her already curvy body, more so. She needed a halter to hold the 'girl's' up, as she likes to call them. Charlie is so beautiful, but still has some issues with accepting and believing it. She is not fat by any means whatsoever. She's got curves that I would kill to have. I'm as skinny as they come; you could use me as an ironing board, and I'll never understand what made her dad say those hateful things to her. They simply aren't true. He's such a douchebag and if I could get my hands around his neck I'd….

I don't get a chance to finish my thought before I hear, "So, really, this looks okay?"

"Girl, Maverick is going to eat you up like a Popsicle. You are hot Char, don't you dare even second guess me on this."

"You know T, I don't want to embarrass myself, but if you're sure..." I know how hard this is for her, and I'm certainly not a heartless bitch. Buying the bikini was a huge step for her. I know wearing the bathing suit wrap will make her feel better.

Baby steps, right?

"If it will make you feel better, I will concede and you can wear the wrap." I see a huge look of relief on her face that she doesn't even attempt to hide.

"Are you sure? I mean a bet is a bet and I did make a deal," she sputters out. The fact she was willing to go without it, is enough for me.

"Nope, grab it. You'll feel more confident with wearing the two-piece and I love the confident Charlie. You'll get there girl. Mark my words."

She walks over to me and gives me a hug and says, "Thanks T," and then heads out of my room.

Before she's completely out I ask, "Charlie, you know I've always got your back, right?"

She turns, cocks her head to the side and smiles, "Duh."

I can't help but laugh out loud at her, because she just pulled my signature mannerism. She knows exactly why I'm laughing. That is so completely what I do all of the time.

I'm a head cocker. Well, that sure didn't sound right in my head. Note to self, never say that out loud, ever.

I shake my head and close my door, knowing I only have about an hour before we leave and I need to mentally prepare myself. I always have to do this when I know I'm going to be around Will. It's so hard. I see how he looks at me and I'd be lying if I said I didn't like it, but I also see something else there. Buried beneath the surface, is hurt. I can see it even through his attempts to hide it. I'm attuned to him more then I'd like to be. I sigh knowing full well that I'm lying to myself, yet again. I would love nothing more than to be completely and utterly attached to everything Will. Sadly, some things are just not meant to be. I lie down and snuggle into the softness of my bed, holding my pillow a little too tight, praying I can lay down for just a few minutes with no thoughts of anything bad. Trying so desperately to clear my head, I finally fall asleep. Unfortunately, instead of dreaming of just Will, I end up with a nightmare.

I see Will and he's staring at me intently until he begins to turn and walk away. I can't seem to move and realize someone is holding me back. My stomach falls to the ground, because I know who it is. I see him in my head every night when I close my eyes begging for sleep to take me, but just once without a nightmare to follow. I don't dare turn around. Crying out, I reach out my hands to grab hold of Will, but his face looks so sad. He doesn't reach for me either, which makes me scream even louder for him. "Will! Will!" I scream with all of my might but he doesn't seem to hear me and completely turns around and begins walking away. Please God, let me wake up. I know what's coming, I know what happens and I can't relive it. I can't. I'm sobbing and I can't seem to stop screaming Will's name.

All of a sudden I'm being shaken, "Tori, wake up, wake up. It's just a dream. You're dreaming."

I slowly open my eyes to see Charlie hovering over me with a look of fear plastered on her face. *Holy shit, it was just a dream. Just a dream, it's not real. Just a dream. I say to myself like a mantra, over and over.*

"Tori, you're scaring me, please say something."

I release the death grip I still have on my pillow which reveals cramped up fingers from holding it too tight. "It was just a dream Char."

"I don't think so, Tori. That was more like a friggin ass nightmare. Are you okay? Do you need to talk about it?"

"Nope, I'm good," and I try to smile to let her know I'm fine so hopefully she won't press me to talk anymore. Disbelieving and irritated, she studies me intently, but says nothing else.

"What time is it? Is it time to go meet them?"

She releases an irritated sigh, but letting it go, turns to walk out. "Yep, get your skinny ass up and get ready, it's time to go."

The second she closes the door, I crumple into a heap and try to compose myself.

It seemed so fucking real. I need to get a grip. Why, all of a sudden, are my nightmares getting worse?

Knowing I don't have long before she comes back in to get me, I pull my bikini out of my drawer and begin to get ready. I throw on my cut-off jean shorts and slide my feet into my flip flops. Throwing the door open I holler at Charlie, "Did you grab towels and a cooler?"

"I've got it packed up already. Let's go, and I'm driving!"

I will not argue there, I love her Jeep. With the top down and the radio blaring, it's the perfect spring break and summer time vehicle.

I walk outside and see her already in the Jeep with the top down, placing the ever coveted iPod into its place.

"You're not excited are ya?" I tease her, I can't help it. I love seeing her so happy and I'm doubly happy that it's with Maverick. He's such a good guy and so good for her.

Just when I think she's going to ignore me, she gives it right back. "Now, if we can only see you just as happy and excited."

I try to brush her words off, "I am happy." I turn and look out the right side of the car, where the window would be, if the top was on.

"Tori, I want to see you excited for a guy. I want to see you just as freaking giddy as I get when I get to spend time with Mav."

It's always cute when she uses his nickname, but I hate it when she says it to Maverick in front of me. It may as well be just the two of them. Maverick gets this heated look in his eye when it's used and I feel like some kind of voyeur, or pervert. Like I'm intruding on a very private moment, which I'm sure I am.

We pull up to 'their' spot, which will always be deemed "theirs" and get out. I notice Will's truck and not Maverick's, which I'm sure means they rode together.

Grabbing all of our stuff we head off in search of the guys. As soon as we make it to the clearing, there they are and I'm rooted to the ground. Standing before me is the most exquisite male body I've ever seen. He's slim but muscular and he's all Will and perfect. Charlie grabs my hand, pulling me along and gives me a very noticeable look that clearly says, "Uhuh you like him, admit it."

In response, I shrug my shoulders and give her a small smile that says, "What? I'm human and I'd be stupid not to think that's hot."

The moment we get close, Will looks up and stares at me. His look is penetrating, making my whole body feel like it's on fire. It's always like this when I'm around him.

Note to self, there is no preparing for this. You can't, it's impossible.

"Hey ladies," Maverick says.

"Hey Maverick," I say without ever taking my eyes from Will.

Shit, I was staring at him this whole time.

I try to play it cool, maybe he won't notice. "Hey Will. How ya been?"

"Since I talked to you this morning, great. Even better now that you're here," he says with a twinkle in his eye, and wearing a come hither look that would have most girls panting and fanning themselves. Well, I'm definitely not most girls.

Charlie whispers in my ear, "Play nice," before heading over to Maverick. He's staring at her and I see the instant he notices her two piece. Yep, score! He likes it, just like I knew he would. My eyes follow Charlie as she wraps her arms around his neck immediately and it's as if there is no one else around. I begin to feel slightly uncomfortable, and my eyes betray me and stray back over to Will.

He's staring at me with this look of complete desire. I know he's liked me for a while, but this look is new. It's a look of determination, like he's come to a new conclusion of some sort. This look of his scares the ever-living snot out of me and makes me want to go running for the hills in the opposite direction.

I've always been attracted to Will, but he scares me. Not a bad scare, but a good scare; although I guess that depends on how you look at it. The kind of scary you could get lost in and give yourself completely in to, and I can't handle that. My heart, my head and my broken body just can't handle it.

I force myself to tear my eyes away from his, head off closer to the lake and lay my towel down, knowing full well he's watching me walk away. I peel my shorts off, laying them down on my towel and grab my suntan lotion. I swear it feels like my back is on fire from the heat of his stare. I attempt to ignore the scorch that's enveloped me so completely and go about applying my lotion, when I feel warm breath cascade across my neck.

It scares me so badly that I turn around screaming and punch the shit out of the person. Unfortunately, that person turns out to be none other than Will. I'm immediately horrified and feel so ashamed of my behavior. He just stands there and I see no condemnation on his face. "I'm so, so sorry Will. I didn't know it was you," I sputter. I grab at my towel and start to put my shorts back on.

Then I see Maverick and Charlie running towards us shouting and asking what is wrong. They stop in front of us and spot Will's face. "What happened and why does Will have a mark across his cheek?"

I look down at the ground knowing full well there is no explanation that I can give them. Will immediately pipes up saving me, "It's not her fault. I startled her and it was an instant reaction. Truth be told, she's got a mean right hook." My eyes shoot up from the ground and look at him, not sure of what I was expecting, but I know it isn't this.

Charlie suspiciously looks from me to Will and then back to me and I see her eyes soften. "Are you okay T?"

I nod my head that I am and try to put on a brave face, hoping I haven't ruined the day completely for everyone. "I am, again I'm really sorry Will." I hope my eyes can relay how very sorry I feel.

"Think nothing of it, really, it's okay," he says sincerely. Had it been anyone other than Will that I punched, I know for a fact that this would not have been the reaction that I'd received.

I know this first hand.

I know, deep down, that Will would never hurt me, not intentionally anyway.

She's got a mean right hook

Chapter 4

Will

God almighty, the moment I saw Tori come around the corner I couldn't take my eyes off of her. Short cut-offs that showed her long, lean, tan legs with no shirt, only a bikini top; be still my beating heart. I'm sure I looked like a freak staring at her like I did, but I couldn't help it. My eyes were glued to her. I watched her walk away and head for the water and sliding those short shorts off of her long legs. It did things to me, and I couldn't keep my legs firmly planted on the ground any longer. They moved of their own accord.

I ached to touch her and I was done with just looking. I wasn't doing anything wrong, right? I would just be helping to rub the lotion in. I made my way over to her, and I think the freak in me might have inhaled her, when I reached her, causing my breath to fan out across her neck. She smelled so good, like strawberries.

Unfortunately, her reaction wasn't what I was expecting, because the next thing I heard was a scream, and I felt a hard smack right across my cheek. Well, I've never received a response like this from a girl I'd gotten close to. All joking aside, the moment I opened my eyes and looked at her, all I could see and sense was fear. Unwittingly, I completely terrified Tori. I don't know how, but I sure as hell wanted to find out. A girl doesn't react that way without a reason and several different scenarios were flying through my brain.

Seeing Maverick and Charlie come running at Tori's scream made me feel like shit, and she immediately started to apologize. Honestly, for what? I was the idiot who sniffed her and scared the ever-living shit out of her. I could tell she felt horrible and embarrassed, and I was trying to put the whole situation to bed and let it go. I didn't want her to feel weird around me. That's the last thing I wanted.

I tried to laugh it off and tell her what a mean right hook she had, which I hoped helped to lighten the atmosphere just a tad. Obviously concerned, Charlie just watched Tori. Witnessing their interaction, told me a couple of things. One, Charlie was just as concerned about Tori, and two, she had no clue what was going on with her either.

Charlie being in the dark is extremely concerning. If Charlie doesn't know why she's acting this way, then Tori's hiding something. This isn't the Tori we all know and that worries me. My mouthy redhead seems to have disappeared and I aim to get her back.

Experiments

Chapter 5

Tori

Thoroughly embarrassed, I am determined to let it go and have a good time, but it will take some major pretending on my part. "Hey Char, do you have your iPod on you?"

"You silly girl, when do I not have it on me?" She tosses it to me, so I can put it on the player and crank it up. Charlie and I have a lot of differences, but the one constant similarity is that we both love our music. We love all kinds of music, but thank goodness that girl loves country music as much as I do, or we might have had a problem.

I chuckle and shake my head, grateful the whole 'incident' is forgotten, at least for now. I begin grabbing food out of the cooler and glance at Will, hoping to make this less weird between us. "Will, want to help me get this food out? We can eat first, lay out and then get in the water? I may even let you help me put on my suntan lotion." I toss a wink over my shoulder at him for good measure.

Did I really just say that? Holy shit, do I have diarrhea of the mouth or what? What happened to the cool Tori that was suave and didn't say stupid crap all of the time.

As I finish completely cussing myself out internally, I turn around and find Will, right beside me with plates in hand. "I didn't want to startle you again, but I did say your name. You seemed somewhere else. Are you sure you're okay?"

"No, I'm fine, thanks. I was just thinking," I whisper to him. Once again, I begin getting completely warm all over from his nearness. He and I pass out the food, like a team. It's silly, but something as small as passing food out together to our friends feels so natural. I know, I'm so crazy. Maybe that's my problem; I'm going nuts.

While we eat, Charlie and Maverick keep the conversation going with Will and I only chiming in here and there. I notice the looks he's giving me, and I can't help but look right back.

I decide to throw it out there and go for broke. I jump up, grab Will's hand, surprising everyone, and hand him the bottle of lotion. I walk him over to the towel and turn my back to him. Before I can move my hair back, he brushes it to the side and whispers, "Is this okay?" Sighing, I barely manage a slight nod of my head. He carefully and gingerly begins to apply the sunscreen to my shoulders. And I thought his nearness was a lot to handle! Not only is he so very close, but his hands elicit a feeling in me that I haven't felt in a very long time, like at least a year. I force my mind to go somewhere else, and not back to that night. I close my eyes and just feel, telling myself this is a good touch; one I could possibly get used to. I feel his hands move in a circular motion, first down, then back up around my neck. Who knew Will had the most perfectly skilled hands? He puts more lotion in his hands and gently moves it down my arm, all the way down to my fingertips, almost holding my hand, then reversing the movements back up my arm. My breathing starts to get heavier as he moves on to my other arm, repeating the experience exactly; all the way down to my fingertips. Only this time, he does hold my hand, keeping it at my side, and finally speaks, "Was that okay, did I apply enough?"

Are you kidding me? I want to scream and say it was so perfect, and you made me feel things, and hell no! I need more lotion! One application is definitely not enough. But of course, I don't say a thing. I'm so affected, I'm afraid to even speak. All he did was apply lotion but shit, it feels like more. So much. More.

I finally croak out, "Thanks, that's good." I am so smooth, I tell ya. As I turn around, I see Charlie and Maverick giving us a stare down. Technically, Charlie is catching bugs with her mouth wide open, and Maverick has his traditional "Maverick" look going on; one eye brow raised, perplexed, and his expression saying, "What the hell and what did I miss?"

Clearing my throat, I stand up and shake the sand off of my legs. Turning to everyone I ask, "Are we going in, or what?" I smile so they think I'm totally not affected, run to Charlie and yank her by the arm pulling her along with me. Laughing, we run into the water, just like kids. We turn around and look at the shore to discover the guys are nowhere to be seen. All of a sudden, I hear Charlie shriek and see Maverick grabbing her from behind, wrapping his arms around her waist. I watch as she rests her head on his shoulder while he places a kiss on the side of her forehead.

Something in me feels damaged and not whole, like I'm missing a part of me. I feel so sad all of a sudden. I love how happy Charlie is, but I want that too, and I honestly don't see how I can ever have that for myself. Will's head finally pops up, out of nowhere, and I'm proud of myself for not slapping the dickens out of him again. Did he not learn with my earlier response?

"Before you say anything Tori, I did holler at you, but you didn't respond. You seemed to be deep in thought, again. You're doing that a lot lately. Anything you want to talk about?"

"Nope, no talking." And I do something I'm sure I'm going to regret, but I'm calling this experiment number two. I throw my arms around his neck and run my fingers through his soft hair at the nape of his neck, and start pulling him near me, but he pulls back, stopping me from following through.

"You should know, if we do this, it will change everything." He cautions with the most serious expression that I've ever seen on his face. I don't even care right now, all rational thoughts fly out the window. All I know is that I have wanted him for over a year, and I have to try this, for me. I gaze straight into the depths of his gorgeous eyes, before I grab his head and plunge forward. The kiss starts slow, like he's wanting to feel everything, not wanting to miss a thing.

I can handle and do this.

I'm feeling hot and tingly, and decide to sink a little deeper, and kiss him even harder and more frantically.

Suddenly, flashes of a past memory move to the forefront of my mind, and I'm revisiting it all over again.

Both of my hands are being gripped tightly by one strong hand, pressing them into a door handle of a truck. My legs are pinned down, with a knee pushed between them, holding me in place. Bites--they aren't even kisses. They're just bites, making my lips bleed and I can taste the blood. I'm wrenching my head back and forth, desperately trying to keep him from touching his grotesque lips to mine. He finally makes contact with my lips, and I feel the urge to purge every ounce of food from my stomach, but it doesn't happen. I try with all of my might to scream and cry NO! But I can't get the words out. His mouth is either on me, or his putrid smelling hand is across my face, silencing my screams. His hand begins to snake its way down my stomach and all I can think is, God No. Please No, not like this.

All of a sudden, the flash is over and I see Will, right in front me, looking scared. Tears are running down my face, and I move my hand to my lips, and I'm shaking all over. I'm so damaged, I can't even kiss a guy, a good one at that, without breaking down like a nutcase. I glance at Charlie and Maverick who, thankfully don't witness my breakdown, because they don't come running. I look back at Will, "Please, can you take me home? I need to go home."

Will just nods his head and begins walking through the water, being careful not to touch me. Like a crazy person, I start to laugh. I tell myself it's the insanity coming out; I knew it would happen. I'm shaking so hard I can hardly walk out of the water and up the bank, but I don't want to be touched. The laughing finally subsides and turns back to tears. I make my way up the trail and we reach his truck. He opens the door and I slide in, still soaking wet.

Will grabs a blanket out of the back seat and comes back around to my side. "I don't want to startle you, but I'm going to put this around you, okay?" Teeth chattering, all I can do is nod my head in understanding. Using extreme caution and care, he wraps the blanket completely around me, never taking his eyes off me.

He gets in and we ride in silence, and it's heartbreaking. I'm no longer sobbing uncontrollably, but silently crying. I'm crying for every shameful thing that was done to me. I'm crying for the loss, and for my mistake. I'm crying for everything that has happened, and that will never happen. Because the loss is more than anyone will ever know.

He pulls into the driveway and chancing a look at him, I utter two small, but very significant words, "I'm sorry." He will never know what those words mean to me.

He doesn't say anything, because what is there to say? He steps out of his truck, showing the gentleman that he is, walks to my side, and opens my door. Downcast, I quietly get out, not wanting to look him in the face, ever again. I don't think I could bear it.

Leaving him standing at the truck door, I walk to the front door, chiding myself for being such a coward, allow myself one more glance at him before the door is closed. I look directly into his eyes and see a look of pure anguish pasted across his beautiful face. It's the last thing I see, before I shut the door.

The moment the door is shut, I hear my mom, "Is that you, Tori?"

Trying to keep my voice from betraying me, I clear it quietly and reply, "Yeah mom, Charlie is with Maverick and will be home later."

"Okay Tori, love you baby girl."

Trying to keep myself from breaking down all over again, I quickly respond with, "I love you, too, mom."

Making my way upstairs and while clutching Will's blanket tight around me, I catch a whiff of his cologne,

I hadn't noticed before. Instantly, my insides tighten and I take a long inhale of it, hoping to capture the smell forever and store it in my memory. I reach my room and drape the blanket across my desk chair to dry. I grab my night gown, go into the bathroom and undress to take a shower. I stop to glance in the mirror, and take a good look at myself and recalling the night I came home a year ago. I touch my fingers to my lips, to my cheek, then to my ear. I repeat this process without even realizing I'm doing it, while tears cascade down my tortured face. I bring my hand down and along my throat remembering the 'love bite's' he so enjoyed calling them. I run my hand down my sternum, to my breast, where they were tortured painfully; a place I don't think I could ever handle anyone touching me, ever again. I wrap my arms around myself, not wanting to remember, or go down my body any further. I don't want to recall anymore. I just need it all to go away.

I get in the shower and scrub, trying to wash every feeling he made me feel that night, down the drain. As hard as I try, I know deep down I can't. Look where trying to forget has gotten me? I was successful for a time, but things have a way of catching up to you. Why? Why now, has my past chosen to come back and haunt me?

Finally giving up, I turn the water off, grab my towel and get dressed. I walk to my room noting that Charlie still isn't home. I realize it's still light outside. Hell, it's not even dinner-time, but I feel drained and I'm tired.

I fear he'll be there when I fall asleep. Maybe I can make myself dream of Will. Sweet, gorgeous, Will that makes me feel like everything will be all right. Even though I know it never will be. As much as I try to keep my eyes open, I can't, and sleep finally wins and pulls me under.

Safe in my arms

Chapter 6

Will

I thought I was going to die when she reached over wanting to kiss me and I certainly wasn't joking when I said, it would change everything. Because it did, and in more ways than one. Kissing Tori was unlike anything I'd ever experienced. Her lips are so warm and soft and fit perfectly with mine. When she deepened the kiss I thought I was in heaven. Until she suddenly stopped kissing me. Her lips just stopped moving; like she was in shock. I pulled back noticing that something was wrong, and watched as a look of pure torment crossed her gorgeous face.

I have never in my life felt as damn helpless as I did in that moment. It was like watching a silent movie and seeing moments of pure terror cross her face, as the tears cascaded their way down. It was heart wrenching, but I couldn't get her back, until she came back to herself.

I was terrified of causing her any more pain by placing the blanket around her, but she was shivering and her lips were chattering. Wrapping my blanket around her was the only thing I could do. In a stupid way I felt it was my arms wrapped around her and I was helping, if only in the smallest of ways; I was keeping her safe.

Driving her home was excruciating. I've never felt so protective of someone that wasn't family, Maverick or Charlie. I knew she was trying to hide it, but she cried the whole ride to her house. When I opened her door I wanted to say something. Something that would make her feel safe and she would know I was here for her. I needed her to know that I'd always be here for her. But the words wouldn't come out, and truth be told, I knew there wasn't anything I could say to make her feel better.

Deep down, I knew that something bad happened to Tori. I didn't know what, who, when or where, but my gut was telling me that she had to have gone through something so horrendous, to cause her this much pain.

Somehow, I needed her to know that I wasn't going away. I'm in it for the long haul. I just hope she will let me in when she is ready.

Biting Kisses

Chapter 7

Tori

I'm dreaming of Will and he's standing right beside me. We're at a party with a ton of people, and he says he's going to go get us a drink. I remember smiling up at him and feeling so happy that he finally asked me out. Shit, it took him long enough, I thought to myself. I remember giving him one of my signature smiles that most guys can't resist. Like pressing pause, everything stopped in the room, everything but me. I glance down and notice what I'm wearing, and instantly, fear trickles down my spine as I remember this is no ordinary dream. This is my worst nightmare and I begin to recall everything from that horrible night.

I'd had a drink prior to Will picking me up, something to give me just a little bit of courage. I've liked him since the first time I met him. There was just something so charismatic about him, and he was just an all-around good guy. I swear I felt chemistry the very first time our eyes met and I was sunk from there on out. So yes, I had a little liquid courage. I wasn't drunk, but I was feeling good; I felt great in fact. I felt like I could handle anything. Will left to get us drinks and I walked outside—which was the worst and one of the stupidest mistakes I have ever made.

I was approached by a guy. He was tall and good-looking, but I wasn't interested in him. I'd never seen him before and I knew he didn't go to our school, he had to be older. He looked to be in college and seemed shocked that I didn't want anything to do with him. I didn't, I had Will and was waiting for him, and I said as much. He threw his head back and laughed as if what I said was the funniest thing he'd ever heard in the world. I felt a sickening fear, and my instincts were telling me to run like a bat out of hell. I told him I needed to go find my date. He latched on to my arm rather tightly and started to walk us towards the back of the property where a bonfire was blazing high. Trucks and cars were scattered around it, and I kept telling him to let go; that my date would find me. But I felt weak; just when I'd needed my strength, it was all gone. All because I needed to have some extra 'courage' and now when I need my strength it's gone.

He was too strong and I couldn't budge from his grip. I tried. Oh God, did I try. I was so terrified I started to scream and yell at him to let me go. As we'd passed by people, they'd all laughed, like it was funny. They were too plastered to see what was right in front of them, that something wasn't right and I'd needed help. He'd gripped my arm even tighter causing my vision to blur and tears to start welling up in my eyes. I was trying to be strong, not just physically, but I wanted to be strong and show him I wasn't scared. I didn't need this guy to see my fear; people like him live on it and get off on it. I was trying so hard to be strong, but then I got weak. I failed.

Pulling me in front of a truck, he'd opened the door, yanking me in while I was kicking and screaming. He pulled so hard my arm had felt like it was being pulled out of the socket, and the pain caused my vision to blur. The moment he got me in his truck, I knew I was done, but I never stopped fighting, and I never stopped saying no. He'd quickly locked the doors and tossed me hard across the bench, and held my hands over my head with one hand. I could feel the door knob digging into my wrist. I will never, for as long as I live, forget that feeling.

He continued holding my hands with one of his giant hands as I thrashed around and he attempted to kiss me. His idea of kissing turned into 'biting kisses', his term for them, not mine. His breath was rank, a mixture of cigarettes and cheap alcohol that gave me the urge to throw up the entire contents of my stomach. His 'biting kisses' turned extra rough. He bit my neck, my ear, my throat and then made his way down to my shoulder. He eventually made his way back up, where he was determined to capture my lips. The rougher he got with his determination, the more blood I started to taste inside of my mouth. I started to feel absolutely no hope for a rescue and I started to give up, until he started to make his way down to my breast. He grabbed them in his rough hands and squeezed so hard I saw stars and continued with his 'biting kisses' as he made his way down my body.

I laid there silently crying and he must have thought I had given up because he loosened his grip. I got a hand loose and I slung it up over my head on the glass. Laughing at me, he grabbed for my hand once again and subdued me with a cruel slap across my face and said, "You want it and like it rough, don't ya? You're a little fighter you are. I knew having a red head would bring some spice." I winced at his words, and I felt the blood trickling down the side of my face, I felt like I was dying on the inside. My fight had just about left me.

All of the sudden I heard a familiar voice calling out for me; it was Will. I went nuts and my fight returned. I thrashed, and pushed, and tried to budge, but I couldn't seem to gain any purchase. He laughed quietly and said into my ear, "This is going to be so much fun and makes things so much more exciting, don't you think? He's right there, and I have you right here." Will's voice moved further and further away, and before long I couldn't hear it at all.

His hand started to make the treacherous descent down my waist, when I remembered I was wearing a skirt, which made me cry even harder. He took his hand and roughly threw it over my mouth, squeezed my cheeks painfully in the process and told me to shut the fuck up. I did as he demanded and hoped that if I did, things may not get that bad.

Deep down I knew it's over for me. As I laid there praying to God that help would eventually come, he whispered in my ear as his hand started lifting up my skirt. "You're so beautiful. I noticed when you first got here and I knew I had to have you." This made my tears fall even harder.

By the end of it all, when he was finally done with me, the truck door opened and I was finally allowed to leave. I stumbled out of the truck, too damaged and broken to feel anything. I was numb.

Physically and emotionally in pain, I realize how ostracizing this experience was: you can only understand if it's happened to you. And it's a feeling I wouldn't wish on my worst enemy. Things were done to me that night that had never been done before and I will never, ever forget, and I've never told a soul.

Numb

Chapter 8

Tori

I wake up from the nightmare screaming 'NO' over, and over. I open my eyes and spot Charlie sitting in the chair beside my bed, a look of concern etched across her face, as she chews on her thumb nail. My mom lays beside me, trying to sooth me, like she did when I was a child. She wipes my hair away from my face that's sticky with wet tears, and I can't seem to stop crying. My mom whispers soothing words into my ear until I begin to calm down.

When I'm finally lucid she says, "Tori, I know something's going on with you and I need to know what it is. I've noticed for a while, but I really didn't think anything of it, until recently. You need to tell me what's going on. I'm so worried about you honey."

Charlie stands up looking sad and quietly says, "Maybe I should leave for this? I mean, I'm not really family anyway."

Mom responds, "No, you live in this house, and you are family whether you realize it, or not. The moment you moved in, you were mine; blood or not. I love you, Charlie, and I know Tori does too. This is a family matter, and girl you're our family." Shelby looks at Charlie with love and tears pouring through her eyes and smiles kindly at her.

I find my voice, not wanting Charlie to leave. She needs to know as much as my mom does, and I honestly don't think I have it in me to repeat it a second time. "Charlie, you are my sister in every way that matters, not just my best friend, and as hard as this is going to be to tell you, it's important that you know."

I take a deep breath. This is it. This is my defining moment. I have to tell them, and I'll see the same shame that is etched across my face every time I think about that day, even a whole year later.

I begin my horrific nightmare. Charlie immediately moves and slides in with me, offering a piece of her comfort. I start at the beginning when Will first asked me out and how absolutely excited I was. But also how incredibly nervous I was. I tell my mom that I drank something right before Will picked me up. I tell her about Will leaving to get us a drink, and how I went outside for some air. I tell her about the foul smelling guy and go into detail with the 'kissing bites.' I hear an audible gasp escape Charlie's lips, but ignore it and continue. I tell her about how I fought hard, and vehemently said no.

"I did momma, I tried really hard, but he was too strong and I couldn't escape him." Tears continue to track their way down my face and I feel a soft hand gently rub them away. If only it were that simple, to just rub your demons away and be whole again; if only.

I hear mom whisper words in my ear, but I don't know what they are. I can't make them out, there's just too much jumbled in my head. I hear that she knows I'm a fighter, at least that's what I think I hear, or maybe it's what I want to hear.

Taking a small breath I continue recalling my nightmare. I laugh bitterly, picking up my hand for a closer inspection, and turning it over to show them, holding it in the air. "This hand will never be the same ever again. Every day, for the rest of my life, I will forever feel the truck handle being embedded into the back of my hand. My hands were held down by one of his strong hands while he used his other hand for other things. Shit, it's only a hand for fuck's sake and it will never be the same. Just think, anytime a guy wants to hold my hand, I'll feel the itching begin and then the itching will turn into a sharp, digging pain. I can look at my hand and physically see there isn't anything wrong with it, yet there is. I'm damaged beyond repair and I will never be whole."

My mom stays silent; quiet tears run down her face.

Charlie's arm tightens on my arm, but I can't look at her. I'm trying so hard to be strong, but if I take a chance and look, I will completely break, and lose it, and there is so much more to tell.

Transported to another time and place, I remember as if it happened this morning. "I heard Will, calling me from the distance, and I tried to make as much noise as possible. But then he slapped me so hard I saw stars and tasted blood." As if this wasn't bad enough, and hard enough to tell, I tell her about the end and how, after he was done with me, I was discarded like trash. "He opened the door and told me to get out, and pushed me until I stumbled out of the truck and fell, landing on my hands and knees." Once again, I pick up my hands inspecting my palms but see nothing. I remember them being battered and dirty. I scraped them when I fell. I remember them hurting.

Dead silence; that's all there is, and I'm all talked out. There's nothing left of me.

When I'm done with my tale, Mom sits still as night, tears glistening but with nothing of what I expected. There is no judgment appearing on her face, only love, showing bright, and true. I also see pain, and I know she weeps for what I've lost, and for my internal pain that I've held in for all this time.

Suddenly, she bolts up and begins to pace the room. Anger pours off her in waves, and I can tell she's desperately attempting to reign in the outrage that is wafting off her. "Tori, we have to go to the police, we have to do something! He can't get away with it! He hurt you, baby, and he needs to be punished," she says as tears trickle down her face. She stops pacing and stands stock still, just looking at me waiting for me to say something, anything.

The thought of going anywhere right now freaks me out. It's hard enough to tell my mom and Charlie and the thought of going into a police station sends me go into hysterics. "Mom, I don't know who he is and I don't know his name. I know nothing and this happened a year ago. I waited a whole year before I said anything. What do you think they are going to say? It's hopeless, so hopeless." I sob out at her.

Defeated, she looks down at the carpet and rubs her hands over her eyes before crawling in bed behind me, wrapping me in her arms, just like she used to. She asks me something so unexpected, "Is this okay?"

I nod my head, but it causes me to hyperventilate. She's so worried about touching me, and my reaction; a mother should never have to ask if she can hold her child. This makes me feel worse. "Tori, I've got you and you are safe baby." She says with a slight tremor to her voice.

I finally glance at Charlie, seeing her eyes so full of emotion for me, tears threatening to trickle down, trying desperately not to let them fall. I know Charlie, she didn't want me to hear her cry and make it worse for me. If she only knew that she couldn't. I feel dead and numb, but finally not quite so alone anymore. She nods her head towards my hand, silently asking me if it's okay. I manage a slight nod, my head feeling too heavy to hold up anymore.

My mom begins to softly sing me a song that I've always loved. One she would sing whenever I got hurt, or I was upset: Fleetwood Mac's *Landslide*.

As she sings to me, I listen to the words reverberate through her chest and close my eyes, listening to her husky timber voice. The same voice I received that mirrors mine; my love of music coming directly from my mother, and passed down to me.

I fall asleep in my momma's arms, listening to her sing and, for the first time in a long time, feel content and safe.

The fight

Chapter 9

Tori

Please no, no, please, I scream out as loud as I can. I see my tormentor up above me and the horrible grin smeared across his face that says this is a game and this is his idea of fun. My insides are churning and I can't get away. My hands feel like they're in a vice and I'm stuck, and oh my God, the back of my hands hurt, they hurt so badly. He's holding on to them for dear life with one strong, large hand. The more I move and thrash, the more he tightens his grip, smiling his evil grin.

All of sudden, other thoughts come rushing to the forefront of my mind. Like, why did I have a drink? Why did I feel like I had to in order to be comfortable with Will? I never had to before with any guy, so why him? I start to hate myself and cuss myself internally while this monster starts discussing his 'love bites' and marking my skin and how much he's going to love seeing his mark all over my body. I'm such a fucking idiot, why did I drink? As I cry harder, the more he enjoys this game of his. I tell myself I need to find a way to calm down, as hard as it's going to be.

But then I hear a voice, and I swear it's calling my name. The voice gets louder, it's Will. He's calling for me, looking for me. I begin to squirm, attempting to scream for him when I am slapped so hard, my face is thrown to the other side. I feel a trickle of blood, and then I taste it. Tears cascade down my face as I begin to crumble piece, by piece.

"Will, come back!" I inwardly scream. Please come back; I'm here, I'm right here. Why don't you look harder for me?

Then I feel a hand begin to snake its way down, and my body begins to revolt from the touch and I can't do a thing to stop it. It feels like a million spiders crawling down my body to my furthermost private area. When he begins to yank my skirt up, I fight even harder and then I scream and I scream until I'm hoarse and I fight to the very fucking end.

"Tori, Tori please wake up baby, It's just a dream, it's not real I promise. You're safe and you're home." Then I hear her whisper, "I would take this all away from you baby if I could, I swear I would."

I hear my mom call for Charlie, "Can you grab me a warm towel, Hun? Thank you."

I can't open my eyes, they feel glued shut and heavy and my throat feels raw, like I've been screaming my head off. Above all, I feel completely battered, not only on the outside, feeling the bruises that have been gone for a year, but on the inside as well. I don't want to talk. I have nothing to say, as I continue to rehash this nightmare over, and over. It won't go away; then a sob tears out of my mouth, and I turn my head away from the voices.

I hear Charlie walk back into the room, and warm fingers turn my head. I let her, because I don't care anymore. A warm towel wipes its way across my face in gentle strokes, then carefully around my eyes allowing them to finally begin to open; the light is blinding. I get out a muffled and hoarse whisper for the light to go out. They seem to understand, and turn it off.

"Tori, I know you can hear me. We need to get you help baby, and, by God, we need to find out who this boy is. He needs to go to jail and pay for what he's done. You need to talk to someone, you can't do this by yourself."

I don't say anything because what can I say?

That's a damn joke... Nobody will believe me anyway. I'm the fucking idiot that drank. I wasn't strong enough to fight off my attacker. I screwed up completely and look what I've done. I've ruined my life. What makes her think anyone is going to give two shits about me? Hell, I don't even give two shits about me. It doesn't matter anymore; I don't matter anymore.

"Tori, I know this is hard baby, you've been carrying this for over a year by yourself. Guess what baby girl, you're not alone anymore. You can't handle this on your own. It's impossible. You have to get up. I need you to get up. Something triggered this memory somehow and I don't know what. What I do know, is you can't keep reliving these nightmares." My mom begins to get choked up and says with conviction, "I love and miss my Tori. My Tori is strong, and has a 'take no bull shit from anyone attitude' that you got from me. My Tori is strong willed and doesn't get down on herself, or beat herself up. My Tori loves fiercely, and stands up for others, and fights for what's right and by God, I want her back. So you, Tori, are going to fight. You are going to fight because I need you, and because Charlie needs you, and because you need you to be." Her voice rises with the last part, "Do you hear me?"

I can only nod my head, because I'm choked up by her words, and don't know what to say. What can I say, really?

I miss me too.

Chapter 10

Will

This might just be the dumbest thing I've done today, or ever for that matter, but I was worried about Tori. I had this need to make sure she was okay. I tried calling Charlie, but she never answered. I spoke to Maverick, and he just said he'd spoken to her briefly. Something just wasn't right.

So here I am, parked right outside her house, as I continue to contemplate, do I stay and knock on the door, or do I just put the truck in drive and wait to hear from Charlie or Maverick? Making up my mind, I tell the coward lurking around me to take a hike, and muster the nerve to walk to the door.

Standing at the door, I gently knock, still concerned that I'm disturbing someone. The door quietly swings open, and I see a very bedraggled Ms. Easton, Tori's mom Shelby. Tori is a younger version of her mom, but they look more like sisters than mother and daughter.

Plastering a smile on my face I ask, "Hi Ms. Easton, I just stopped by to see how Tori is? She didn't seem to be feeling well when I dropped her off the other day." I know that's putting it mildly, but it's still true and I don't want to alert her to anything that Tori may not want her to know.

Turning around, she looks back in the house, grabs the doorknob and shuts the door, leaving the two of us on her front porch. She's scaring me and my heart starts to beat double time out of worry. She looks at me tiredly, letting out a deep sigh before beginning to speak, "Will, there are things I can't and won't discuss with you. It's not my place to say anything. The only reason that I'm telling you this much is because I know you care about her. Just know, this needs to come from her, and she's not in a good place right now." Her eyes begin to glisten and she wipes her eyes with her hand, trying to keep the tears at bay.

I don't know what to say. I feel powerless. I knew she wasn't good, but I didn't expect this. I never thought I would see Ms. Easton look so beaten down. Then I realize there is only one thing that I can truly offer her. Clearing my throat and hoping that I don't sound like a dumbass and I come across as sincere, because I am. I've never been so sincere and honest in my whole life.

"Can you give Tori a message from me? I would love nothing more than to deliver it in person, but I think it'll be okay coming from you. Would you please tell her...?" My voice begins to choke up and crack with all of the emotions that I'm feeling. "Please tell her I'll always be here for her, in any capacity, and, and, I've never stopped caring for her, even from a distance."

Tears fall down Ms. Easton's face with my last words. She takes another swipe at her eyes and lays her hand on my shoulder, when I turn to leave. "Will, I will tell her. And thank you. Thank you for caring about my daughter."

Without even thinking, the words just pop out of my mouth, "Tori's easy to care about, and truth be told, I've loved her for a year." This last part comes out as a whisper as I turn to leave, not knowing when I'll get to see, or talk, to her again. I don't turn to look at her again; I just walk away. I walk to my truck and climb in. I watch her go back inside and shut the door. I feel the urge to look up and when I do, I see Tori standing at her window, like a ghost with her hand pressed firmly on the glass, as if to say good-bye.

I watch her until she finally turns away. The thought of not having Tori in my life at all, hurts more than I can bear. It's not a thought I wish to entertain. I need my Tori, I need my mouthy redhead back. I don't know what's wrong, but I need to know what I can do to fix it, and if I even can.

Not until she's completely gone from my sight do I realize my hand is on the glass of my window.

Pissed off

Chapter 11

Tori

As I watch Will walk away and get in his truck, a million feelings burn through me. My hand, of its own accord, touches the glass of my window. Seeming to sense me, Will looks up and sees me standing here. For a moment, I swear my heart stops. A look of sadness fills his face. I don't know why he's sad, but it breaks my already broken heart in two. I watch as his hand mimics my movements and he places it on the glass of his window. I remain there for just a moment before forcing myself to walk away, afraid he'll 'see' something just by the look on my face. As if telling my secrets has left me exposed for all to see. Do I appear different? Can anybody tell what I've been through just by looking at me? I know these are silly questions, but they run through my mind nonetheless on a consistent basis.

I turn around and walk to my bed, knowing my mom will be up shortly. Just as I finish the thought, I hear a light knock on my door. "Tori, that was Will and he has a message for you, which I think you really need to hear."

I tentatively say, "Okay." I clench my hands together in anticipation for whatever it is that had Will so compelled to tell my mom something so private.

Taking a deep breath she says, "He wanted me to tell you that he'll always be here for you. But more importantly he wanted you to know… he has never stopped caring about you, not even from a distance."

It takes her one good look at my face to see I need a few minutes of alone time. She steps out of the room, shutting the door and granting me some much needed privacy.

Tears lightly stream down my face, because these are words I wanted to hear a year ago. I care about Will a lot, but I never know how he feels. Sure, I'd catch him looking; that wasn't a new thing. Guys often checked me out, this isn't me being conceited. I know my height, frame and my blasted strange colored hair get me noticed. But I never wanted another guy's attention on me, only Will's. I wanted his piercing green eyes to see me, and only me. I wanted to shiver when I heard him say my name because it caused sparks to ignite, just from the timber of his voice. I wanted Will to eventually be my first. The last thought causes me to choke on a sob, until I'm crying and hitting my pillows and screaming. "Why, why?" I have no other words to say that make any sense; only why.

I cry for the loss of a first time. I cry for the loss of a first love with which to share a first time. I cry because something was taken from me, something that wasn't his to take.

My door opens and I know someone has come in. I feel a familiar voice begin to sooth me before she touches me, her way of preparing me. Charlie wraps her arms around me and I hug her back with all my might, needing her like never before. She uses one of her hands to rub my back in a circular motion, telling me that everything will be okay; that I'm not alone.

My crying begins to ease off and I realize, in this exact moment, I can't do this anymore; I'm sick of crying and feeling scared. I'm tired of feeling broken, and accept there are things that have to happen if I'm going get any better and put this behind me. I have to move on. Not for anyone else; for me.

I lean back and look at Charlie, "Can you go get mom please? I have something I need to say, and I really need to say it to both of you."

"Of course, be right back," she says before walking out the door. Not a minute later, she and my mom rejoin me in my room. I hold my head up for the first time in days, my shoulders up and my back straight, hoping to gain some confidence with what I need to say, and do.

"I know I need to do something, and I can't continue to cry anymore, I can fight." I think I've finally finished the crying stage, at least I hope so and now, I'm starting to just get pissed. I feel broken and I'm tired of feeling this way, but I know I can't do this on my own. I need help. I am finally admitting I need help. I come to another realization. "The truth is, mom, we may never know who the guy is. I never knew his name."

They both watch me carefully waiting for me to continue. But on my mom's face, I see a glimmer of hope begin to rise up and take its place, shoving the gloom aside that's been there for several days.

"I need help with these nightmares. I can't live in fear of falling asleep, and constantly waking up bawling my eyes out. You were right mom, I can't do it alone."

My mom and Charlie simultaneously walk over to me, throw their arms around me, and give their love and support. *I can do this*, I tell myself. *I have my mom and my sister right here to help me along the way, I will do this!*

The epiphany

Chapter 12

Tori

My mom made an appointment this morning for me to see a counselor. Today is also my last day of spring break and I'm spending it in therapy, who'd have thought? Oddly enough, making some difficult decisions that put me first was actually very freeing. I feel like all these burdens that I've been carrying don't need to be mine alone anymore. I have a family that is willing to help carry these burdens with me, and I feel lighter. I know Will and I need to have to have a talk eventually, but I am definitely not ready, or prepared for that, yet. One step at a time.

It feels good to get up, take a shower and get ready to go somewhere with no secrets lingering, or hiding anymore. I'm nervous as hell about going, but my mom's assured me I will be fine. On top of seeing a therapist, who I'll be seeing every week, but I'll also be attending a support group. The group scares me more than the one-on-one with the therapist. I'm not very keen on sharing my story with others, especially when I had a hard enough time sharing it with those I'm closest to.

The second we arrive my stomach flops to the ground, I begin to sweat and I'm shaking like a leaf. *Maybe this wasn't such a good idea. Who am I kidding? I have to do this.* With my decision made, a small spark of the old Tori begins to peek through. It's small, but it's there; I can feel it.

Wiping my hands down the front of my shorts, I look to my mom for assurance and she grabs my hand. "You'll be fine Tori, don't worry. I'm not saying it's going to be easy, but I do think it will help." Taking a deep breath I exit the car and walk to my destination, albeit a little slowly. I am in no rush to begin what I believe will be a torturous experience.

Standing at the door I turn to see my mom still parked, sitting in her car watching me. She gives me what I assume is a small attempt at a reassuring smile, but to me she still looks concerned and maybe a little heartbroken. Facing the door again, and taking a deep breath, I turn the knob, knowing the action will lead me back to my nightmares I've been so desperately trying to avoid.

One last glance back at my mom for good measure before I pass through what is sure to be the threshold of my impending doom. I shut the door behind me and stop, making no move to continue walking.

I command my feet and legs to start moving but they want to stay firmly planted to the ground.

Get a grip Tori. Okay feet, start moving!

Miraculously they become unglued and continue on to our destination. I walk up to the reception area, and as I approach, an older lady sitting behind the glass partition lifts her head, revealing a kind face.

"Hello there, do you have an appointment?"

I feel like I have cotton mouth and I can't seem to force any words out, and barely manage a slight jerky nod of my head. I start breathing heavily and feel like I'm going to pass out. Light headed, I bend over at the waist and begin to shake all over.

I hear a voice say, "Oh dear," and footsteps move closer to where I'm standing.

I feel hands begin to touch me and I let out a blood curdling scream, "Don't touch me! Please God, don't touch me." I begin sobbing uncontrollably, and I can't stop. This is too much, too fast.

I barely register another set of shoes in my blurry vision and the next thing I know…

I wake disoriented, feeling dizzy and not sure where I am. Attempting to sit up, I notice I'm on a rather hard coach.

"Careful, you might be dizzy, and if you get up too fast you might make yourself sick." It's a female voice I can't recall. "I'm sorry, but I had to give you something to calm down. We couldn't calm you and you wouldn't let either one of us touch you. I'm Dr. Heart and you must be Tori?"

Barely registering a nod, I can't help but smirk a little. *Heart, how appropriate; when mine feels like it's been shattered into a million pieces, I wonder if she can fix it.*

"Why are you smirking Tori? My name? Let's talk about that."

Feigning confusion I ask, "What do you mean?"

"You smirked when I told you my name, why?"

I feel kind of bad for doing that, but I don't think she's upset with me. She seems to genuinely want to know. Taking a deep breath, and telling myself it can't hurt to talk just a little bit, and I'm already here. I begin to speak, "Your last name is Heart and mine feels broken. I just thought how appropriate that I would come to a therapist with the last name Heart."

She looks at me thoughtfully. "Why does your heart feel broken, Tori?"

Well shit, what do I have to lose?

I look her straight in the eye and say, "Something bad happened to me and I feel battered, bruised and broken. Not only does my heart feel broken but as a whole I feel beaten and battered."

"How long ago did this happen to you?"

"A little over a year ago," I tell her.

Dr. Heart looks at me and I can see wheels turning, but I have no idea what she's going to say and ask.

"You haven't always been feeling like this have you?"

I decide to just go with it and continue. I can do this and I'm slowly feeling a little more comfortable. She's not looking at me like I'm crazy, in fact the opposite. She looks at me with compassion, as if she really wants to help. So I take a leap. I take a leap of faith and plunge head first into the very depths of my very broken soul.

"You see I had a date with a special guy and I needed a little courage, so I drank a little before we left. I wasn't drunk and he never even knew I had drank anything. We went to a party. Will stepped away to get us something to drink. I was stupid and went outside to get some fresh air because I was warm. Probably from the alcohol I had digested."

Before I can say anything else she asks, "Why do you think you didn't tell anybody about your rape?"

I cringe at the word and have never used it. That word has never escaped my lips.

She notices the cringe, "Tori, you do realize that you were raped, right? What happened to you is and will always be, rape. Without you going into any detail of that night, which we will explore, but not today, you were raped. The way you reacted in the waiting room was enough confirmation."

I sit, listening to her say the word 'rape' several times with tears cascading down my face, once again. All I do is cry and I'm so sick of crying and in this moment I have an epiphany: I. Was. Raped. I've never been able to say the word, or admit to myself I was raped. I knew what happened to me was wrong, but I'd never said I was raped. As this begins to finally sink in, Dr. Heart begins to speak again.

"Is the reason you never told anyone you were raped, because you had a drink of alcohol prior to Will picking you up?"

I look at her and softly say, "Yes."

"Tori, a drink of alcohol, doesn't make this your fault. This was never your fault."

I absorb every word Dr. Heart says and absorb it like a sponge.

"This is all we are going to explore today. I would like you to come back on Tuesday to see me, but I think it would help to go to a group session on Monday. Is that okay with you?"

"Yes," I say. "I think it would."

I left my first session with Dr. Heart feeling, for the first time in a long time, everything might eventually be okay. Maybe there's hope for me, after all.

Guilt is a powerful thing

Chapter 13

Tori

My mom and I don't talk the whole ride home, nor do we talk when we get home. I think she senses that I need the space. I will come to her when I'm ready. I head straight up to my room, my head filled with so many conflicting thoughts, like a sensory overload of some kind. There are things I need to process and they can only be processed by me. No one else can do this for me, as much as I know they wish they could.

Charlie isn't home when we got there; she's probably out with Maverick. I'm glad she's enjoying her last day of spring break, she deserves to be happy, and I've taken enough of her time this week. I never in a million years thought this was how I would spend spring break my senior year of high school. Of course, I never thought I would have been raped, either.

Just thinking the word 'rape', causes chill bumps to erupt on my arms and legs. My mouth starts to get a bitter taste, and I feel frozen in fear sitting in the one place I should feel safe; my room. I lay down pulling my comforter over me and grasping at my pillow like a life line; the way I've done all week since I finally broke. My body starts to shake with what I now understand to be fear, and I close my eyes begging my mind to shake it off. Closing my eyes doesn't help, it only makes things worse, and flashes begin to appear in my head, just bits and pieces. I see a flash of pearly white teeth inside a mouth with a sinister grin attached to it, and evenly matched pair of wicked eyes. For as long as I live I will never forget those eyes.

Like being controlled by a DVR remote, my flashes begin to fast forward. It stops at my fight and when I struggle to get one hand loose and slam it against the glass above my head. Roughly pulling my hand back down and holding it again in his strong grasp, he smiles his sinister grimace enjoying this more than any human being should. Then I'm fast forwarded to the moment I hear Will, calling me and I'm pleading and screaming for him to please find me. I don't feel the slap this time because I'm rewound back to the beginning, when he first found me. I see myself standing innocently, enjoying some fresh air when I'm approached. The whole thing plays out and I can see my struggle and his fingers that dig into my arm yanking and pulling me roughly.

I throw my eyes open as understanding begins to dawn, and a new feeling begins to creep through my body as I realize something so very crucial and evident.

Words begin to echo throughout my head. *I couldn't have fought him off, even if I never had anything to drink. He was way too strong. I was never going to get away from him.*

I begin to cry as the guilt that I've carried and buried inside of me for over a year slowly starts to seep away. "It wasn't my fault," I declare, solely for myself. The moment those words leave my mouth I discover I need to say them to someone else. I want to scream and cry it from the rooftops. The more I say it out loud and think it, the more I'll believe it.

I jump from my bed feeling more energy than I have felt in a very long time and run out of my room searching for my mom, "Mom, where are you?" I frantically call out.

"Tori, what's wrong baby?"

Meeting me at the bottom of the stairs with concern written across her face, I look at her and pronounce, "It wasn't my fault."

Her eyes grow big as she sucks in a breath, letting it out while tears begin to trickle down. "No, baby it was never your fault; never." Opening her arms wide open, I rush into them feeling a small weight slowly being lifted off of me. I hug her with all my might while I cry tears of relief.

"I felt so guilty mom, like it was my fault. I kept telling myself if I never drank anything, then it wouldn't have happened. I would have been stronger, and I could have fought him off."

My mom pulls slightly away and places a hand on each side of my face, looking straight into my eyes and says, "Tori, there is absolutely nothing you could have done to prevent the horrific things that happened to you. You just happened to be the girl that monster picked out that night. If it wasn't you, it would have been another victim."

Without really thinking, and with more strength I've had in a while, I blurt out, "Mom, I don't want to be a victim, and I certainly don't want to be his. I am nobody's victim!"

Hugging me to her she whispers in my ear, "You, my girl, are a survivor, and you will get through this because you are mine and you are strong as hell. You have a fire in you that nobody can ever put out, unless you let them, and don't ever let anyone put out your fire."

I pull her as close to me as humanly possible, "I love you, mom."

"Oh Tori, I love you more than you will ever know."

Shittin ass truck

Chapter 14

Will

I have not been able to think of anything else but Tori since the day I stopped by her house.

Shit who am I kidding? She's always on my mind.

The conversation with Tori's mom replays over and over in my head. Watching Tori in the upstairs window with a look of complete and utter helplessness kills me inside. I toss and turn in bed wondering what I'm missing because something tells me that I'm missing something crucial.

I let out a deep sigh and wonder what I can do.

Finally giving up, I call Maverick, not caring about what time of night it is. The phone rings several times, but just when I'm about to hang up, I hear a very groggy voice.

"Hello?"

"Maverick, its Will."

Maverick clears his throat, "What's wrong, everything alright?"

"No, it's not," I sigh. "I have some things I need to talk to you about. I keep thinking about things, and nothing is making any sense, I just don't know…"

Maverick interrupts, "Why don't you start at the beginning."

Because I know how Maverick feels about Charlie, I don't ever have to worry about him judging me. He just gets it and understands completely. Taking a deep breath I lay it all out.

"Well at the lake…"

Maverick sighs and interrupts me again. "No Will, at the beginning. How about starting at the very beginning, the first date you never talk about. You've never spoken about that night. I've always wondered, and I've asked you but you wouldn't tell me so I didn't push you. What did happen?"

I take myself back to that night over a year ago.

"You know I'd been crazy about her for a while, and I'd finally gotten the balls to ask her out. I was nervous as hell like a pansy ass, but she didn't even hesitate when I asked her, which took me completely by surprise. Like the generic lame ass person I was, I decided to take her to a party. You remember that huge party Ty had when his parent's went out of town?" I don't even wait for him to answer before continuing on, lost in the memory.

"I picked her up and she was so excited see me. God, she was gorgeous. She had this hot short denim skirt on with a tank top that hugged her curves just right. I remember thinking how lucky I was that she would be at the party with me, and no one else. As soon as I parked at Ty's, she tried to open up her own door. I put my hand on her bare knee to stop her, and I swear, just innocently touching her made sparks fly, at least for me they did. She just looked at me and smiled her sexy grin. I got out, walked to her side and opened her door. That smile never left her face. As soon as I shut her door, she reached over and grabbed my hand. That's how we walked into Ty's house, hand in hand. When we walked in, we continued holding hands and it felt like we were there as a couple. It felt amazing."

I take a second to remember that feeling when Maverick pipes up. "What happened then? What changed? It seems like everything was going great."

I sigh loudly and lay down on my bed. "I don't know. I looked at Tori and asked if she was thirsty and she smiled, nodding, saying she could use a drink. I swear she wasn't really talking about the drink. I will never forget the look in her eyes when she said that. I left her there because it was so crowded, and I went to get us both a drink. I was held up by some of the guys on the team, and when I went back, she was gone. I looked all over, I called for her everywhere, but I couldn't find her. I guess it was maybe, I don't know thirty minutes later when I saw a truck door open in the back by the bon fire. All I know is when that door swung open, she was sitting there. Shocked, I quickly spun around and immediately walked away. I never went back. I figured she'd find her own ride home and didn't need me. I guess I read too much into how I thought she was feeling about me."

As I lay there thinking, Maverick begins to speak, "Wow, I couldn't even begin to imagine how I would feel if I was in your position. I can't imagine what I would've done if it were me and Charlie and I'd seen her get out of some dude's truck. I know that it would have killed me to see that. I'm sorry bro. Why didn't you ever say anything to me?"

That's a good question, I tell myself. The only explanation I have is I guess I was embarrassed and I kind of wanted to forget about it and pretend it didn't happen. The sad thing is, I will never forget that. It felt like my insides were being ripped in two.

"I don't know Maverick, I guess I was ashamed."

Maverick doesn't say anything for at least a minute and we sit there in silence. "Dude, you had nothing to be ashamed about, but the thing I don't understand is that I saw how crazy Tori was about you, and what you saw doesn't make any sense. You know she's not like that. She's never been that kind of girl. But I can see how you felt that way, I'm sorry man."

"It's just that none of this makes any sense. I felt deep down that we were on the same page, at least I thought we were." Shaking my head to clear it I say, "I just don't get it."

"I talked to Charlie, Will, and I know that Tori seems to be going through something but she said it wasn't her place to tell me. Tori's tough, so whatever it is, it doesn't sound good. I know you still care about her, I can see it every time you see her. You do still like her a lot, right?"

I don't even have to think about it. And it's not just like, and hasn't been for a long time. "I never stopped caring about her and wanting her. Just being around her causes every feeling I've ever had for her to come roaring back. Even after seeing her come out of that shittin ass truck, my feelings never changed. I'm a glutton for punishment, aren't I?"

"No Will, you love her. People make mistakes all the time, but that doesn't mean you stop loving them. You really need to talk to her about it, if you want to entertain the idea of being with her."

"I tried; I went over to her house." I tell Maverick about the conversation with her mom.

"I know I need to talk to her. I guess I'll see if she's willing to talk to me at school on Monday."

I thank Maverick for being a good friend, for talking to me in the middle of the night, and for listening. I lay in bed after hanging up, just thinking. It feels good to have talked to him about all of this, now to do something about it and talk to Tori. If she'll talk to me, anyway.

Put a brave face on

Chapter 15

Tori

Monday morning came way too soon. My nightmares are still here but I'm beginning to manage them a little better. My mom gives me the go ahead to stay at home, but I decide to go to school. I feel this deep need to keep things as normal as possible, and stay on a regular schedule. However, the thought of seeing Will not only terrifies me, but my stomach does flip flops anticipating being near him again. It's strange how you can feel fear and anticipation at the same time.

I have a group session today after school, my first one. I'm extremely nervous but mom, Charlie and I have been talking about it. They think that by hearing others talk about their own experiences will help me. I don't know, I'm undecided.

I come down the stairs to hear Charlie and my mom whispering. Unfortunately, eaves dropping doesn't do a bit of good because I can't hear a thing. I stand in the foyer and stare at myself in the mirror. So many things start moving through my mind.

Will anyone know? Do I look any different?

I think the thought that scares me most of all, is how is Will going to act towards me? I know that this past week has changed everything and I can't bear to have him look at me different. Staring at myself, I don't seem any different, but my eyes look tired, and they have dark circles under them even makeup can't hide.

I hope and pray I can do this without causing a huge scene, and I can at least act like the old Tori.

I barely register Charlie's reflection come up behind me in the mirror, when she asks, "Are you okay? Are you sure that you are ready for this?"

Not wanting to alert my mom, I turn to her and quietly say, "Honestly, no, but I don't think I'll ever be ready. If I don't dive in, head first, and do this, I don't think I ever will. We only have a month and a half left, right?"

I've been going to school since I was raped--the word itself igniting goose bumps to chill me all over, making me shiver.

But since I've begun to come to grips with my reality and everything is out in the open with my family, in my head it feels like going to school right after it happened. It feels fresh, and raw. I can't explain it. It's like being raped all over again. As I replay the last statement in my head, I realize it's true.

"You ready to go?" Charlie asks me.

I snort, "Sure. Let's do it and get it over with."

The moment we get in her Jeep and she starts driving she asks, "I know this is a very sore subject, T, but when are you going to tell Will?"

Sadness takes over and crashes through my entire being. I glance over at Charlie, "I know I'm not ready for that just yet. I've just now come to grips with what's happened to me."

She quickly glances at me with a look of understanding.

Continuing on I say, "I know he probably thinks I'm crazy as a loon now, considering how I've reacted and everything."

Charlie sighs and says, "No T, I think you will be surprised. Will's not the kind of guy to be scared off easily." Quietly she says, "I think he cares about you more than you realize."

A thought quickly runs through my head. *"If that were true, wouldn't he have talked to me after that night? At least asked me what happened?"*

As we pull into the school parking lot, I feel my courage begin to quickly slip and start to rethink this going to school thing.

"I don't know if I can do this Charlie."

She grabs my hand, squeezing it, not realizing what that small amount of simple comfort does for me; giving me just a little bit of her strength.

"Tori you don't have to, you can stay home, even for another week."

I realize no, I can't. I have to do this impossibly hard thing for me. I have to put a brave face on and go in there. Hiding at home and not speaking to anyone isn't going to help me at all.

"I got this Char," I say.

Taking the biggest breath I swear I've ever breathed and pasting a small smile on my face, I look at her. "Okay, let's do this."

I open the door and slowly close it, prodding my feet and legs to move forward. Oddly enough, they do. I meet Charlie at the tail end of the Jeep and she loops her arm through mine.

Glancing around I ask, "Where's Maverick? He's never not here standing at his car waiting for you."

"Um, I thought this was something we needed to do together."

I glance at her nervously as she rushes out, "No T, I didn't tell him. I just said that you and I needed some time before school started and he didn't press. He said he would see me later."

I glance at my best friend who's become a sister in every way that matters and I can't help but feel so grateful to have her in my life.

As we trudge forward and near the senior lounge we begin to see students and classmates talking amongst themselves. I begin feeling nervous and scared, and my steps begin to falter, and then I see Will. He's surrounded by several of his fellow football players, and Maverick.

As if sensing me standing there, he looks up and our eyes catch. A look of indecision crosses his face, but he decides to walk over.

"Are you going to be okay?" Charlie asks.

"Yes, I am, I need to talk to him. Not about the 'other thing', but he and I still need to talk. I can't ignore him forever."

"Okay if you're sure. I'll go and see Maverick then. If you need me, just signal and I'll come right over."

I don't get a chance to thank her before Will's standing in front of me. She gives my arm a squeeze, and walks over to Maverick. I watch as his eyes light up when he sees her and wraps his arms around her waist, pulling her to him, then kissing her sweetly.

I turn to look at Will seeing a very similar look in his eyes, but mixed with something else.

"Hey, can we talk for a minute?" he asks.

"Yeah, sure." I say and follow him out to a quiet place in the courtyard.

As we stop, he turns to me and looks at me intently.

So many emotions swirl around, and inside me. I glance up and look directly into his face. A face I could have once lost myself in, and stared at for hours.

He clears his throat. "I came by, did your mom tell you?"

I nod my head and force words to come out. This is so much harder than I thought it would be. "She did."

"'I've been worried about you Tori, are you okay?"

I think hard before I answer, "I will be. I'm not yet, but I will be, *eventually*."

He lightly nods and turns his head to the side looking somewhere past me.

Finally turning back and looking me straight in the eyes, he asks the one question I'm dreading and know deep down is coming. "What happened?"

Forcing myself to breathe in and out and not go nutzoid on him I murmur, "I can't tell you yet." I turn my head away and look out at nothing in particular. I can't say this and look at him just yet. "I want to, I really do, but I'm not ready yet."

After a few moments he abruptly speaks, "Tori, please look at me." I hear the pleading in his voice and it breaks my heart, so I give him that. I turn my head and stare into the very depths of those deep green eyes that caught my attention so long ago.

He lifts his hand up to place it on my cheek, but thinking better of it, he lowers it back down. The funny thing is, I didn't flinch. It's Will, and I know he would never hurt me. The truth of this causes something inside me to loosen, and I feel a bit triumphant.

Sighing he says, "Did your mom give you my message?"

I know what he's talking about and I'd give anything to hear him actually say words to me.

"She did."

"I just want, no I need you to know that I mean it and…"

Before he can finish, I surprise even myself when I say, "Say them to me, please."

His eyes grow wide then soften. Walking a little closer to me he asks, "Is this okay?"

I feel like an emotional basket case, and my heart is beating so fast at his nearness. It's scary, but I'm not scared. His kindness and tenderness towards me makes me feel cherished in a small way, and I simply nod.

He's whisper close when he says, "I've never stopped caring about you, not even from a distance."

I close my eyes, as tears begin to trickle slowly down my face. I never thought I would hear these words come out of his mouth, and I allow them to sink into the very center of me. I've felt such guilt and shame I didn't think I deserved to hear anything like this, ever again. I open my eyes to see a tender look on his face, meant only for me.

"Thank you. Will, I needed to hear that." I don't know what to say to let him know I care, but I do something so shocking and unexpected, even to me. I take my right hand and place it lightly on his cheek, just to feel something good. He leans into my palm and closes his eyes, doing things to my heart.

My heart actually begins to beat again. Not in fear like I've been so used to, but for life. It beats because this guy, who's been so patient with me, still cares. But the most terrifying part is, I realize I want him too.

The bell rings and Will's eyes open. We stand there for just a moment longer staring at each other before pulling apart. Throwing me a lop-sided grin he asks, "Can I walk you to your class?"

"I'd like that." I smile back.

We walk in silence to my class, but before walking in, I turn to him and promise, "We'll talk later."

He smiles that hopeful grin and jams his hands into his front pockets as he begins to back away, all the while watching me walk in. I can still see him when I take my seat.

He pulls one hand out and gives me a little wave and a smile before walking to his class.

I sit and contemplate the time he and I talked, or just stood there, more accurately. I can't squelch the fear that begins to creep in as I sit thinking this is all fine and dandy, but what happens when I do tell him? Will he see me as used and damaged? He's a good guy, too good for me actually. Doesn't he deserve to be with someone who doesn't have all the emotional garbage I have? Someone he doesn't have to ask permission to move closer, or even touch?

The teacher begins talking, cutting off all of my thoughts and I decide to quit worrying and focus on school.

Yeah right, school. Because that'll be easy.

Hope

Chapter 16

Walking to my class is harder than hell. I want nothing more than to grab her and hold her. I want to tell her that whatever is hurting her I can help. I honestly don't think there's anything that would make me not want her.

I reach my class a little late and sit down in my seat across from Maverick, who has an eyebrow raised at me in question. I just nod my head at him and face forward.

I hate the tortured looks that cross her face. Walking over to her when I first saw her this morning, I knew I had to talk to her. It hurt when she said she couldn't talk to me and tell me what was going on, but I won't let this deter me. I have a gut feeling she will eventually explain, I just have to be patient.

When she asked me to tell her I cared about her, it took everything in me not to pull her close to me. I knew I couldn't, but God I wanted to. I could sense she needed to hear it, but until that moment, I didn't know what effect my words would physically have on her. Watching her close her eyes as she absorbed them completely was nearly my undoing, until I saw the tears. The tears practically killed me.

I could see the courage it took her to reach out and place her palm on my face. There aren't even enough words for me to describe how her touch affected me. I swear I felt a shiver run through my body, down to my toes.

Lord that smile. I saw a small smile appear on her face, and it was the first genuine one I'd seen in a long while reach her eyes, and I didn't want to look away. I had to force myself to turn around and walk across the hall to class.

I know, whatever I do, I have to tread carefully. Seeing that smile and feeling her touch and hearing her words is enough to instill a glimmer of hope.

I glance over at Maverick. He turns and looks at me, throwing that same damn eyebrow up again. I should tell him if he doesn't quit that shit, his eyebrow's going to be stuck like that. The thought causes me to chuckle quietly and shake my head.

"Anything you'd like to share with the rest of the class, Will?"

Straightening up and getting rid of any trace of a smirk, I clear my throat by saying, "No, sorry, Ms. Turner."

She glares at me before turning around and I decide I'd better get my head screwed on straight and quit thinking about Tori, which proves to be an extremely impossible task.

Survivor

Chapter 17

Tori

Thankfully the day passes rather quickly, and uneventfully. My feelings of concern dissolve away the later the day goes on. I think of Will several times and see him passing by. At one point, Charlie and I stop at her locker and Will and Maverick show up. Will and I didn't speak; there wasn't anything to say. We said everything we needed to, but there were looks; lots of them. The intense looks written across his face every time he looks my way is enough. It is a comfortable silence between us.

The anxiety of my group meeting this afternoon keeps my mind wondering. I'm not sure what to expect and feel concerned about the prospect of having to spill my guts. Especially since I have just come to terms with it myself. I feel like a jumble of nerves, like I have a million butterflies swarming around.

Charlie and I walk out to the parking lot to her Jeep.

"How did you feel about today, T?" Charlie asks.

"It wasn't nearly as bad as I thought it would be. Nobody looked at me like I had the scarlet letter or anything stamped across my chest, thank God."

Charlie can't help but giggle. "Did you really think people were going to think something?"

"I don't know, I just came to grips with this myself, ya know? I don't know how to explain it."

She throws her arm around my shoulders and lightly squeezes it. "I think I kind of get it. I was afraid people would know how I'd been treated by my dad. I didn't want you to know, or anyone else for that matter. I was so afraid of what anyone would think. I know it's not the same thing, but I get it." We continue in silence until we reach the Jeep and get in. "I'll drop you off and wait outside until your session is over. I can do my homework in the Jeep while you're inside."

"You sure? I can have mom pick me up. You don't have to wait on me."

"I'll be fine and you may need me when you're done, unless you want your mom instead?"

"Nope, I would love if you'd wait for me."

"Cool." She says with a pleased smile across her face.

We arrive at a large church where the group sessions are held. I glance at Charlie, "Well I guess this doesn't look too scary."

Grabbing my hand and squeezing it she says, "No, you will be fine. I don't doubt it'll be hard, but you will be fine; I swear."

Feeling her confidence in me strengthens me, and taking a deep breath, I say, "Okay, here goes nothing." I walk towards the church looming ahead, getting bigger the closer I get. I will myself to open the doors working to keep my breathing steady and not wanting to react the way I did at my first session with Dr. Heart; otherwise, this could be humiliating.

Moving entirely inside, I see a laminated piece of paper reading:

GROUP SESSION/RAPE SURVIVORS

Huh, I think to myself, well isn't that just dandy. At least there's no question where I'm supposed to go. I find myself clenching and unclenching my fists. I pull the door open and it creaks, not quietly either. It's loud enough to gain attention from several people who are scattered about the room. I look around and notice a podium table that says 'sign in' here. So that's what I do; I walk over and sign in. I'm unsure what I'm supposed to do next; so I stand there, waiting.

A lady walks over to me. "Hi, you must be new, I'm Claire, the director of the group."

"My name's Tori."

"Well Tori, it's very nice to meet you. I hope you feel comfortable in our group. I'll introduce you when we start."

Before I can even ask the question I'm terrified to ask she continues, "I don't want you to feel you have to share tonight. I want you to feel comfortable before you do. It's important for you to gain some trust first. Does that sound okay to you?"

Breathing out a sigh of relief, I rush out a little too quickly, "Thank you."

"Trust me, we won't throw you to the wolves. We do want you to feel comfortable to share otherwise this group won't work. These girls and women pour their hearts out weekly, and they've gained the comfort level to do so. You will too, eventually."

I look at her dubiously, but she just looks at me kindly and asserts, "You will because talking about it is what you need and this will help you heal."

Before I can respond she says, "Come on and I'll introduce you to some of the girls."

I don't have a choice, so I just follow, as much as I don't want to. I take stock of my surroundings and see a variety of different faces; young and just a little older than me. She leads me to a girl that's shorter than I am with an angelic face and looks around my age.

"Sam, this is Tori. Do you think you could walk her around and introduce to her to the others before group starts?"

I tentatively smile at her as she asks, "Are you nervous?" She has a small voice that matches her face. She has a sweetness about her that makes my stomach clench knowing what obviously has happened to her and it makes me sad.

"That would be the understatement of the century." I say.

"Maybe it'll make it a little easier to get to know some of the other survivor's."

I stop her and ask, "Do you look at yourself like that?" Feeling horrible for asking the question I begin to apologize, "I'm sorry…"

She interrupts me and says, "No, really it's okay and I'm fine to talk about it. There was a time I couldn't. I mean I had a hard enough time accepting what happened to me. I felt so alone until my dad convinced to get some help. My dad, had a really hard time with it for a while, but it's just my dad and me. My mom skipped town when I was young and it's all I've ever known."

I feel shocked at her words and her openness with me. Apparently I'm horrible at masking my expression because she says, "This happened to me a while ago and I've had time to heal. Trust me, I will never forget it, but it gets easier with time and talking about it helps, believe it or not."

I'm awed at her strength. She leads me around introducing me to girls my age, college age and a little younger than me, which breaks my heart in two.

Before I know it, Claire begins to speak and instructs everyone to take a seat. There are about twenty chairs arranged in a circle. I follow Sam, since she's the one I've spent the most time with, and sit down next to her.

"We have a new member with us tonight. This is Tori everyone."

In unison everyone chimes, "Welcome Tori."

I throw a small wave and give a hello back.

"Would anyone like to begin?" Claire asks.

I look around and see several hands shoot up, completely surprising me. I honestly thought we'd sit here for a while, waiting for people to volunteer. Or Claire would call on someone to start the conversation. At least six girls have their hands raised.

Claire calls on a girl named Payton. She's a pretty blonde and looks to be slightly older than I am.

Peyton begins her story. I sit and absorb every word, and every story each girl has to tell. There are several girls with situations very similar to mine, not to mention the guilt some felt and were able to get over.

There are also girls still dealing with the guilt like me, but are willing to discuss it openly. I can see why the sign on the door says survivors because that's what they are. They are definitely not victims.

As I sit here and contemplate everything I've heard so far, I hear another girl, named Tiffiney that I briefly met, begin to speak.

"Lucas, my boyfriend has been really great. He's finally consented to come to some counseling sessions with me."

As she continues to speak I'm flabbergasted. This girl has a boyfriend and he knows about it? And he's still with her? He didn't run?

Without thinking before I do it, I ask, "So, Tiffiney, your boyfriend knows about everything and he gets it?"

"Well, don't get me wrong, he had a very hard time with it; still does sometimes. He hates what was done to me, but he knows it wasn't my fault. He's been with me since the beginning. He gets angry, not with me, but he's really supportive."

I let this information sink in when she asks me a question I didn't see coming. "Do you have a boyfriend?"

I'm mad at myself for opening my mouth, but I need to respond since I'm the dumbass that spoke out in the first place. "Me?" I ask. "No, but there was someone." I stutter a little before continuing, suddenly put on the spot, but willing myself to continue. "We were on our first date." I look down at my hands searching for the strength I need. "We liked each other for a while and he finally asked me out. There aren't enough words to express how excited I was." I don't go into detail because I'm not ready to, yet. "He still wants to be with me, but he doesn't know what happened. I never told him. And I kinda freaked out on him, and slapped him. It all just came crashing back. Can you believe, after all that, he still wants to date me?"

I hear a couple of sighs and look up. Several of the girls exchange looks, and one pipes up and says, "Then he's a keeper. If, after all that, he still likes you, why not take the chance?"

Sighing I say, "Because I'm scared of what he'll think of me." There I said it out loud, and now it's out in the open.

Claire begins to speak, "Don't you think you should give him the chance to make that choice? Telling him your deepest, darkest secret is hard, maybe even the hardest thing you'll do. But sometimes, sometimes they surprise you and end up being the one person you needed all along."

I think about her words throughout the rest of group, say my goodbyes and head out to the parking lot. I'm proud of myself, not only for walking in, but for actually participating.

I walk along and spot Charlie sitting in the Jeep, listening to her iPod--shocker there, and open the door to climb in.

"You doing okay?" She asks.

"Strangely enough, yeah, I think I am."

She smiles, sensing a slight change in me, and says, "Good, let's go home."

The world breaks everyone, and afterward, some are stronger at the broken places.
- Ernest Hemmingway

Chapter 18

Tori

When Charlie and I get home mom has dinner ready. Sitting down at the table my mom looks at me and asks, "Do you want to talk about it?"

I look at her thoughtfully, "It was such an eye opener. I mean, I was scared to even walk in the door, and afraid of repeating my performance when I saw Dr. Heart for the first time. I just knew I would make a fool out of myself. But I didn't. I opened the door and walked in. I'm not sure how to describe it; they were so open about their experiences. I hope I'll be able to get there and be as open as they were."

They take everything in and I see this look of pride cross my mom's face prompting me to say, "Mom, I haven't done anything yet. I don't know why you have this look that says I've done something so huge, when I haven't."

My mom sits up straighter and says in a stern, yet loving voice, "Now see, this is where you're wrong, so very wrong. You not only went to see Dr. Heart, as hard as that was. But you persevered and kept going. You had a good attitude and went to the group, and you took it in and opened yourself up to the experience and gave it a shot and that makes you one hell of a young woman. You could have very easily chosen to wallow and not do a thing about it, but that's not the case. Tori, you are so strong, and doing everything possible to get better. I believe you will get there; I know you will!"

Seeing the faith she has for me, I glance over to Charlie and see the same look reflected in her face. Charlie nods her head in agreement and says, "She's right, you are so strong!" She looks down at the table and then back up to me, "I honestly don't know if I could be as strong as you."

"Are you crazy?" I say. "Look at all you've been through and accomplished. Look how you are today!"

Charlie looks at me, "This is different though T."

I begin, "No, it's not." My tone gets forceful because I know what she went through all too well, and I don't want her to cheapen her experiences. "They may be two different situations, but what you went through isn't any less, different, but not less. Don't make it that way. Don't lessen what your mom and dad did to you. How they treated you was deplorable and they are terrible excuses for human beings." I take a deep breath; rant over.

My mom turns to Charlie, "She's right honey. The circumstances aren't the same, but you've endured a lot. You are so strong and better for coming out of this the way you have."

Charlie takes her turn looking up at both of us, her eyes misty. "Thank you."

"Aw, we love you Char," I say this with her sing-song voice she so likes to use on me.

I continue to share with them about the group meeting, bringing up Tiffiney and Sam. They sit there quietly listening when I say, "This brings me to something else; I'm thinking about the idea of telling Will. I mean I'm not sure I'm quite ready but..." I trail off.

I wait for reactions and, surprisingly, I don't receive any. So taking a deep breath, I press forward, "I like him a lot, and I want a relationship with him, eventually. I know he wants one with me, too. He doesn't make me feel like he would look at me differently; at least I hope not. I hope my instincts are right."

"Well," my mom says, "You know I will support you in any way I can. After having the chat with him that day he stopped by I think you've got yourself a good guy. I am a little skeptical just because I'm your mom, and I don't want to see you get hurt. But I do believe his feelings are genuine."

"Okay, I think I'll ponder on it a while, and maybe discuss it with Dr. Heart."

My mom looks at me thoughtfully, and I see her wheels turning, from the look on her face. "I honestly think that's one of the healthiest things you can do. I think you need to discuss it in depth with her first. Make sure that it is something you're ready to do."

I turn to Charlie because I value her opinion and I know how close she and Will became when Maverick was being a dip shit. "What do you think? Do you think my instincts are wrong?"

"Honestly T, I think Will would be pretty supportive, and I know how much he cares about you. I agree speaking to your therapist is a really good idea, and any guidance sure as heck wouldn't hurt."

That night I lay in bed thinking about everything that had been discussed today, from the group session to my realization that I want to tell Will. This isn't a small thing; this is huge. I would be telling my deepest and darkest secret to the one guy I truly care about. It could go both ways. He could either run for the hills, or he could choose to stay and stand by me through all the weird issues I have, and will probably take a long time to get over. The more I think about everything, the more anxious I become, and questions begin to swirl around in my head until I finally drift off to sleep.

Bile rears its ugly head and attempts to push itself out of my mouth but I swallow it back down. Evil, hateful laughter begins to ring in my ears, a sound I will never forget. My hands are being held above my head and they hurt; they hurt so badly. My eyes are screwed shut. I don't dare open them to see the face of my tormentor. "Don't you dare open them," I say to myself. I'm crying and begging to be let go when I hear a voice. A voice so familiar it brings a yearning to my soul and makes me beg to be let go and makes me fight harder when I feel a slap so hard my head is thrown to the side and something begins to trickle down my cheek. "Please wake up, please wake up," I say like a mantra. I can taste the blood in my mouth. The voice appears to be moving further away, and I cry harder. I feel my skirt being yanked up around my waist. I've lost, I've lost this fight, so I let go.

I wake with a start, sitting up quickly, then jump out of bed. I run to the bathroom and look in the mirror prior to splashing cold water on my face. There are tears streaking down my cheeks and I have blood shot eyes. "I'm safe," I proclaim to myself. The dreams have to start getting easier, right? My heart continues to beat a million miles a minute, and I feel my body shaking.

Standing in front of the mirror, I glance down at my hands. My hands that will never be the same. The same hands that were held down and slammed against the truck door. They tingle and itch; I can't explain it. I begin to have doubts about telling Will. Who would want this? This being the whole 'package' that is me. I'm seeking help the way I'm supposed to, but I'm still damaged and slightly numb. I can, at least, admit the fact that I couldn't have stopped it, but is this something he can handle? Taking one last look at myself I walk back to my room and see Charlie standing in her doorway.

She looks concerned, "Are you okay? Did you have a bad dream?"

I sigh, "No, more like a nightmare."

She gives me a look, "That's what I meant smartass. Do you want some company?"

I feel a sense of relief at not having to go back to bed by myself. Having Charlie in my room with me might help keep the nightmares at bay. "If you don't mind, I would really like that."

She smiles and follows me to my room.

As we climb in I begin to feel a little bit safer, as if 'he' can't get me here, not with Charlie in my room.

What once was broken, might actually be saved

Chapter 19

Tori

No more dreams for the rest of the night, thankfully and the day passes rather quickly, I notice. I've become more of a people watcher since I've come to grips with what happened to me. I see people going about their business laughing and smiling. I see so many different groups of people hanging out, and not seeing anything bad in the world. Most of them will never see or experience the bad, and I hope they never have to. I like to think I will eventually forget some of the "bad" and move on to be at least a fraction of who I once was.

I sense a presence, and quickly look up to see Will across the hall gazing at me intently. The moment our eyes meet, he smiles and walks over. Returning his smile, I feel my heart speed up at the thought of just standing next to him.

"OMG! Get a grip. He's just a guy!"

But he's not just a guy; Will is one of the good ones, and I berate myself for forgetting.

"Hey Tori, I haven't really seen you today. You're not hiding from me, are you?"

I can't really answer his question honestly. I have been, kind of. The truth is he clouds my judgment, and I lose all form of rational thought. I have my session this afternoon and I want to go in with a clear head.

"No Will, I'm sorry, I've just been really busy." I look away so he won't see the lie I'm spewing.

"I'm sorry," he says. I glance at him, his brow wrinkled in deep concentration because this is the kind of guy he is. "Anything I can do to help?"

Feeling like shit I say, "No, but thank you. I appreciate it. I'm sorry to be in a hurry but I've got somewhere I've got to be, and I don't want to be late."

I turn to leave when I hear, "I've missed you today."

I turn back around, look him in the eye and tell him with every ounce of feeling I possess, "I missed you too." I turn quickly and hurry to my car to make my appointment with Dr. Heart. The appointment I am driving myself to. I don't want to take anymore of Charlie's time, not to mention it's something that I need to do myself.

I know I can't continue with this silence, and I know Will needs to be told. In this moment, every fiber in my body is screaming at me that this is worth doing. That he is worthy of my secrets.

I head to Dr. Heart's office, park, and head up to open the door. I don't feel the same way I arrived and have a sense of accomplishment. So much so, I pump my arm in the air like an idiot. But I don't care it feels so huge to me!

I walk up to the receptionist and give her my name as she smiles kindly and informs me it will be a few minutes. Sitting down and grabbing my Kindle out of my bag, I turn it on and begin reading. Not something I get to do often, but it's an escape for me. However, it isn't long before I'm called and Dr. Heart opens her door prompting me to walk in.

"Have a seat Tori."

I sit down on her couch feeling a lot more comfortable than the last time I was here. That was a catastrophe and a half.

"How have you been since your last visit?"

"I'm still having nightmares." I say.

"I'm afraid you'll continue to have them for a while. Everyone's different, but you may have them occasionally over the years until you can push it back. How about your group session? What did you think?"

"Oddly enough it wasn't bad. I was surprised by how outgoing they were with their experiences. I didn't expect it. One of them even has a boyfriend."

"Does it surprise you that she has a boyfriend?"

"Well yeah."

"Why do you think that is?" Dr. Heart asks.

"Truthfully? I can't imagine any guy getting over something so horrible, let alone the guy I really like, at least, not without seeing me differently." I look down at my damaged hands, sigh, and begin to tell her about Will. "I was with Will the night it happened. I liked him for so long and it was our very first date."

"The special 'guy' you talked about at your last session?"

I nod my head yes and continue, "He wonders about what happened to me and he still wants to be with me, but he doesn't know what happened that night. I want to tell him, but at the same time I'm scared to death of telling him."

"You're afraid that he'll see you differently and not want you anymore?"

"Yes," I whisper and look down.

"I think sometimes we can't always heal by ourselves, and sometimes the person who we are most scared to tell is the one person who can actually help us heal."

I listen to that statement and repeat it in my head. It resonates something deep inside me and sticks; it makes perfect sense.

"What event triggered you finally coming to terms with your rape? What were you doing when it finally hit you?"

"We were at the lake, all of us, Charlie, Maverick and Will."

"Had you been having dreams prior to the lake?"

I nod my head, "I actually had one that morning."

"What happened that day to trigger everything to come back?"

Calmly I take myself back, to the day that seems so long ago, but was really just over a week ago.

"I remember seeing Will and wanting him. I flirted and was daring myself to put myself out there. I was pushing the envelope to see how far I could take it. Daring myself I guess you could say."

"What did you dare yourself to do?"

"Well first, Will startled me and I punched him and I was mortified. He didn't mean to scare me. He came up behind me and I reacted."

"What did he say to your reaction?"

"He actually took it really well. He was concerned about me, but he brushed it off; asked me if I was okay.

I said I was and I apologized profusely. But then I really pushed myself to do something big. I called them 'experiments' and I grabbed him and attempted to kiss him, but he stopped me."

In the retelling, I recall something he'd told me. "He stopped me and said, "If we do this, it will change everything.""

"I didn't care and never responded. I just kissed him. We kissed until I started getting flashes of that night, and I just lost it. I cried buckets of tears, but he was patient and never treated me like I was crazy. He got me home safely, even took a blanket and wrapped it around me, letting me know what he was doing so he wouldn't make things worse. He was sweet, and concerned. A couple of days later, he even stopped by my house and talked to my mom. He told her to tell me he never stopped caring about me, not even from a distance."

Dr. Heart begins to speak, "Subconsciously, in your efforts to forget about your rape, you thought maybe connecting with Will could help you forget, but instead, it did the opposite. It actually triggered every memory about your assault. It was never going to go away, Tori. Eventually, you had to come to terms with your rape and face it head on."

She stops talking, giving me time to let this sink in and then I ask, "What do you think about telling Will?"

"That I cannot tell you what to do. You have to decide what's best, and right for you. Deep down, I think you know what to do. I will say this; Will seems like a very nice and level headed guy, who cares a lot for you. He hasn't run from you; in fact he's been there the whole time, waiting patiently."

We talk for another ten minutes before time is up and it's time to go. Before I walk out the door she says, "There is one thing I would like you to do. Find an outlet; something you enjoy and do it. It's a form of therapy, but one that you'll enjoy. What is it you like to do that would accomplish this?"

I don't even have to think, "I love to sing and I used to play the guitar."

"All right, I think that's perfect. I'll see you next week, Tori."

I say goodbye and head home. She's right, I already know what I'm going to do, and it feels so right.

I never stopped caring, not even from a distance

Chapter 20

Tori

I walk in the front door, smell dinner and suddenly realize how hungry I am. My appetite is slowly beginning to come back to me. It's amazing how slaying your demons can bring back your love of food. I walk in to the kitchen to find Mom and Charlie laughing together. It's so nice to see Charlie have a 'mom' relationship with mine. I don't mind sharing, Charlie deserves this and we're lucky to have her. I take a moment, leaning against the door-frame, watching them laugh and talk about their day.

Charlie finally spots me and cocks her head to the side, "You look different T, what's up?"

"I had a good session, came to some realizations, and I have decided to talk to Will. I think it's the right thing to do for me, and maybe for him." I hang my head then add, "Well he may not think so after I tell him, but what do I have to lose, right?" I chuckle because I know what I've got to lose and it's a hell of a lot.

"Why don't you come over and let's eat." Mom suggests. After we sit down, my mom replies, "You know I will support whatever decision you make. I will always stand behind you!"

"Me too!" Charlie says.

Knowing they have my back, I enjoy dinner for the first time in a long time with a lighter heart, but anxiety driven none the less. Before I get up from the table I say, "I'm going to go and call Will."

Deciding to do this and actually doing it are two different things. I'm nervous as hell to be honest, hence the sweat I'm now feeling on my hands as I rub down them down my pant legs. Excusing myself, I grab my phone out of my bag and take it upstairs.

Just do it, you weenie.

I scroll down my phone and see his picture beside his number. My hands shaking, I hit the button that will lead me directly to him. It rings once, twice and then I hear, "Hello?" Hearing him say hello gives me a sense of peace and my trepidation begins to melt away. I'm still nervous, but I feel a little more confident.

"Hey Will, can we talk tonight? Do you have plans? It's time I tell you some things."

With no hesitation, he quickly responds, "No, none. Do you want me to come there or do you...?"

I interrupt him, "No I'll meet you at the lake. I guess at Charlie and Maverick's spot?"

"Okay, meet you there in ten minutes?"

"Yeah, see you in a few." I turn around and spot Charlie.

"I wasn't listening T, I just walked up."

"Charlie, it's okay," I smile up at her.

"Are you sure you're going to be fine driving up there by yourself? Do you really think you're ready to tell him?" Charlie looks at me with concern.

I give her a reassuring smile, "Honestly? I didn't think I would ever tell him or this soon, but seeing him and talking to him at school, and then today's session with Dr. Heart? It feels right. I can't explain it. Now, I'd be lying if I said I wasn't scared; I am, scared shitless, actually. But something tells me it'll be okay, and it's what I need to do. If I have any hope of ever having a relationship with anyone, then I need to be open and honest, and I want one with Will."

My confession feels really good to speak out loud; even better than saying it in my head.

Charlie must agree because she shakes her head at me and laughs, "You know that's the very first time you've actually said it out loud." She turns serious all of a sudden and says, "I want you happy, and you deserve to be happy. I know you won't be magically healed and this'll be a process, but you will be happy."

I cross to her and hug her. No one knows this more than she does. I step back and look down at her, me and my Amazonian height, and comprehend:

Aren't we all just that--a work in progress?

"Okay, I'm going to be late, then he'll think I chickened out."

I take off and get in my car. The whole drive my anxiety is skyrocketing and I'm hoping to hell I haven't misjudged myself. Not to mention what Will's reaction will be.

I pull in and spot his truck and get out. I see him sitting on the tail gate as I walk around my car. For a few moment's I am awe struck. I take him in completely. His disheveled blond hair and piercing green eyes that would root me to this very spot if I let them. But I don't.

As I make my way to him, he watches me intently, searching for something, maybe wondering if this is real, just as I am. I keep walking until I reach him.

Finally he says something and it comes out a little sad, "I didn't think you were going to come."

"Sorry, I didn't mean to be late. Charlie was talking to me."

His delicious mouth curves up on one corner. "Speaking of Charlie, I think it's about time we let them know this isn't just 'their' spot anymore. What do you think?"

I lightly laugh, "I think you're right."

A silence befalls us when he reaches out his hand, "May I?"

I nod my head because there is nothing I want more than to feel his hand in mine. He wraps his large hand around mine, and it feels so fiercely protective and right. He leads us to a spot, and as we approach, I notice under his arm is a rolled up blanket. He catches my glance and quickly says, "So we have a place to sit."

I am such a bundle of nerves and I hope I can do what I've set out to accomplish. This is for me, more, than it is for him. We reach his designated place and he unlocks his hand from mine, briefly leaving me cold and lonely. Laying the blanket down, he grabs my hand again, sensing his comforting touch is exactly what I need to get me through this conversation. He sits cross-legged on the blanket and I follow suit, sitting directly in front of him with our hands holding on to each other as they lay between us.

I gaze out at the water, my heart hammering in my chest. This is it; if this doesn't go exactly how I want, it could break me completely in two. I quietly begin, "I really don't know where to start and I know I owe you so many explanations." My voice hitches; a show of nerves. On a hunch, I look at him directly focusing on his beautiful, honest eyes. Knowing that I'm about to bear my soul to him I take a deep breath and say a quick prayer in my head, and begin where it all started.

"I don't remember ever being as happy until that day you finally asked me out. We flirted for so long and were friends, but I wanted so much more with you. There has never been a guy I wanted to be with, until you." His hand tightens on mine, revealing the effect my words have on him, which give me a little more confidence.

"I was so nervous about our date that I got into my mom's liquor cabinet and had a drink. I just needed something to help give me some courage." He doesn't show any emotion, just listens. "When you picked me up, and we got to Ty's house, I was beyond crazy excited that I was with you. Walking in hand-in-hand felt amazing. For the first time I felt like we were together and everyone would know it. But then you left to get something for us to drink, and I made the stupid mistake of walking outside to get some fresh air. Looking back I will always regret that decision."

Feeling like a coward, I turn my head away from his eyes, knowing full well that I cannot say this while looking at him. I can't fathom the look that will grace his handsome face.

"While you were gone, and I was outside, I was approached by a guy. I didn't know who he was. I'd never seen him before." My voice once again defies me, telling of some of my pain. I feel wetness trickle down my cheek, but I ignore it, fully returning to that night completely and continue with my horrific tale.

"He wanted me to go with him, and when I wouldn't, he forcefully grabbed my arm and yanked me so hard towards the cars. I screamed, but everyone was so drunk they thought it was funny."

I feel his hand tighten against mine, and feel his thumb gently caressing me. My heart feels like it is about to thump out of my chest the further I delve into my nightmare.

"He dragged me to his truck beyond the bonfire. I tried, but I couldn't get away." The tears flow faster, causing my throat to constrict and making it hard to talk, but I will myself on. I glance at Will and see nothing of what I've been so afraid to see. He uses his other hand and wipes my tears away, not realizing what the gesture actually means to me.

"He did things to me Will. I couldn't get away, and, God he laughed at me. But then I heard you calling for me, and I tried to scream even louder and fight harder, but he slapped me." Unconsciously, I've brought my other palm to my face touching it until he covers it with his hand, the same hand he'd just used to wipe my tears. "I tried, I really did. He was so strong, and I thought because I had a drink it was my fault I couldn't get away."

His jaw works hard and I see his eyes spark with anger, but not towards me. No, never towards me.

After what seems like forever, he finally speaks, "You thought because you had a drink it was your fault?"

I nod my head, removing my hand, leaving his hand resting on my cheek.

With a gruffness I don't realize he possesses he exclaims, "Tori, this happened a year ago and this whole time you've been holding it in, thinking it was your fault, because of a drink?"

"Yes." It's all I've got.

I can see the question in his eyes before it comes out of his mouth, "Did he…?"

Interrupting him, I quickly respond, "Yes, yes he raped me."

A string of expletives I've never heard him say, tumble out of his mouth, and his hand quickly flies off of my face, the comfort instantly gone. He stands up and begins to pace, every ounce of warmth instantly gone.

This is it; it's over. I'm used and he doesn't want me anymore. I judged this whole situation all wrong. I'm stupid, so, so stupid.

I hang my head, not daring to see the look on his face. Now that he knows, I don't want to see the look of shame or pity that could cross his face. I can't bear it.

All of a sudden he stands in front of me and kneels back down. I close my eyes and he gently grabs my face with both his hands and lifts it up. His thumbs gently rubbing my tears away and says softly, "I'm sorry Tori. I'm angry, but not at you. I could never be angry at you. Look at me baby, please?"

His gentle voice and use of the endearment 'baby' has me opening my eyes and staring into his. I see nothing but compassion reflected back at me. "I don't want to scare you, but I need to tell you something. First, we are going to find this sack of shit. I don't care, we will find him and make him pay for what he did." His anger is palpable, and his voice quivers.

"Second, and this may scare you and I'm sorry if it does, but I'm taking my chances. I fell in love with you over a year ago and I never stopped. My feelings never faltered, and I told you, "I never stopped caring, not even from a distance. This doesn't change how I feel about you. I love you, Tori, and this isn't going to make me stop or change my mind."

I never thought in a million years that he would still want me, or that this wouldn't change his feelings. My heavy, broken heart has grown a little lighter with each revelation, but with him by my side and no secrets, I feel so much stronger.

Feeling safer than I have in a long time I plead, "Will you hold me?"

Without words, he pulls me carefully onto his lap and wraps his strong arms around me; making this the first time I've felt safe in a male's arms in over a year. I feel protected and cherished; that things are finally starting to look up and will be okay. I nuzzle my head in his neck and breathe everything that is Will into every inch of my body.

We stay like this for a while until it's late and I know I need to get home. We walk, hand in hand, to my car and hug goodbye.

I drive home with feelings I never thought I'd get the chance to explore again, and it sure feels a lot like love.

Blinding rage

Chapter 21

Will

I feel nothing but rage. Complete and utter blinding rage. Rage for what that mother fucker did to my girl and my complete stupidity in failing to protect her.

Why did I not walk over to the truck? Why did I assume she was with another guy and walk away? I couldn't go home and deal with this, so here I am at the lake. I grab at my hair and begin to pull it. I know I'm acting like a crazy person but there aren't enough words to describe how I feel.

I yank out my phone and call Maverick, knowing that he's the one person that can calm my ass down before I do something stupid. With my hands shaking I push the number and stand there until he answers.

"Hey Will what's up? I thought you were meeting up with Tori?"

"I did, I really need to talk. Can you please meet me at the lake?"

"Sure bro, I'll leave now."

We hang up and I begin to pace. I see a large stick resting on the ground and pick it up. I start swatting at the larger tree. I know I'm acting so unlike myself but I've never in my life been as pissed as I am right now in this moment. I don't know how much time has passed since I started abusing that tree until I hear Maverick's voice, "Dude, what did that tree, ever do to you?"

So engrossed in my onslaught, I didn't hear him pull up. Instead of giving a play by play of mine and Tori's conversation I look at him and respond with, "Remember how I told you that I spotted her in that truck and then I walked away at the party a year ago?"

Maverick stands there calm but with a very serious look on his face and nods, "I remember."

"How could I have been so stupid? I could have done something, anything to help her. Hell, that mother fucker could have been in jail right now!" I begin pacing again.

"Will, slow down," Maverick says. "Tell me what happened."

I stop moving and look at him dead in the eyes. "She wasn't there in that truck because she wanted to be, she was dragged in to that truck."

I see realization dawn on Maverick's face, replaced by a look of horror and I continue, "He did stuff to her, horrible things and when he was done with her, he just opened the door to let her out. I just happened to see her at that exact moment so I turned and walked away. I walked away because I thought she was with some other guy. Turns out she was, but she was forced in there. What kind of person does that make me to walk away from that?"

I turn around and hop up on the tail gate of my truck and drop my head into my hands. I feel the weight of the tail gate move and then Maverick's hand on my shoulder. "Will, you can't beat yourself up over this. How is Tori doing?"

I lift my head up and say, "She's dealing with it. She lost it when we went to the lake that day and I took her home, now I know why. She's still having a hard time. I ask her if it's okay whenever I get near her. I don't want to startle her or make her uncomfortable."

Maverick hesitates before asking, "Does she know who the guy is?"

"No, but he was at Ty's party that night and I intend to find out."

"First off Will, you aren't alone in this, Tori's my friend too. This guy needs to be put away and 'we' will find out who this fucker is. I know you want to beat the shit out of him but you can't. Hell, I want to beat the ever living tar out of him, but it won't accomplish a thing." Maverick sighs, "It all makes sense now with how she's been acting. I didn't know, Charlie hasn't said a thing to me about any of this."

I feel tears threaten to fall and I do my best to hold them back and rub my fist against my traitorous eyes. I'm so angry, at the bastard who did this to her as well as at myself for not asking questions and just walking away.

"Why did I ever assume that she would have just hopped in a truck with another guy? I should have known better. She's never been like that. Shit, I've never seen her go out with anyone else."

"I'm not saying this to make you feel worse Will, but she's never had eyes for anyone else but you. You need to get over this guilt somehow and figure out what you're going to do about Tori."

I snap, "What do you mean what I'm going to do about Tori? I love her and this doesn't change anything for me."

Maverick has a look of relief on his face, "Good, that's what I was hoping to hear. I didn't want you sitting here wallowing over what you should have done. If you love her and you can get past this, then you need to be there for her."

I look at him dead in the eyes and say, "This doesn't change a thing for me. This wasn't her fault. I still love her! How would you feel if it had been Charlie?"

His eyes darken as he replies, "I'd want to kill the bastard, but I wouldn't and Charlie would need me. I sure as hell would want to find him though and put his ass away."

Maverick places his hand on my arm, "Right now focus on Tori and what she needs and how you can be there for her. Keep in mind that she told you for a reason so she obviously has some strong feelings for you."

I take it all in and realize that he's right. She needs me to be here for her and she told me for a reason. I feel grateful that she chose me to be the one that she would tell this to, honored even that she would trust me. "You're right. Thanks for coming out here and talking me down."

"No problem bro."

We talk for another hour or so just him and me shootin the shit before he stands up to leave.

He slaps me on the back, "I'm going to head home. Are you going to be okay?"

"I'm not the one I'm worried about."

He nods his head and says, "Yeah, I know."

He walks to his car and opens the door, but before getting in he says, "Holler at me if you need anything. Day or night okay?"

I nod my head and throw my hand up waving goodbye. I sit there for a few more minutes before I decide to go home. I make myself a vow first, I will be there for her in any capacity that she needs me. Second, I will find that son of bitch but I won't let this consume me. I can't, for her sake.

Every storm runs out of rain
- Gary Allen lyrics

Chapter 22

Tori

I pull in the driveway and feel so good, dare I say happy even? I feel safe and protected, a feeling I haven't felt in way too long. My emotions were all over the place prior to telling Will but I feel certain that I made the right decision. I've never felt so cared about and he made me feel precious. I walk into the house knowing full well that my mom and Charlie will be waiting on me to get the scoop. Sure enough the moment I walk in I hear, "So?"

I smile and say, "It went incredibly well. I was terrified at first but being with him makes me feel safe and I knew it was going to be okay to tell him. He was pissed and he looked like he was going to hit the roof at first, but he tampered it down really quickly." We talk for a few more minutes before I excuse myself to go to my room. I walk in and go straight to my closet, open it and stare down at the guitar that I haven't attempted to open in so very long. I loved playing my guitar. In fact, I never used to be without it. It had once belonged to my dad, whom I never ever talk about. It was put away the day he left. It would make me so sad to see it around and I couldn't bring myself to play it anymore. How funny that staring down at it right now isn't making me sad. He is merely a small blip anymore. Someone, I rarely ever think about.

I pull out the worn out case and take it to my bed and open it. Sitting pristine is my once prized possession, an acoustic Gibson guitar. I sigh and my body aches to hold and play it like I once did. I gingerly pull it out and sit on my bed, placing the strap around my neck and begin strumming some cords to tune it. It takes several minutes to get it to where I'm happy with the tuning. I begin playing a song and singing softly along with it. I let myself completely go, my fingers never forgetting how to play. They remember as if I'd just played it yesterday. I get to the chorus of the song when I realize the song I chose is so absolutely appropriate, Gary Allen's Every Storm Runs Out of Rain.

"Every storm runs, runs out of rain. Just like every dark night turns into day. Every heartache will fade away. Just like every storm runs, runs out of rain, it's gonna run out of pain."

I close my eyes and feel every word that comes out of my mouth. I'm beginning to feel okay, like this is a brand new day. I sing until I've strung my last chord when I finally open my eyes and see that I'm not alone.

My mom and Charlie are standing in the doorway with misty eyes. My mom comes forward joining me on my bed and Charlie walks across the hall to her room, shutting her door.

My mom says, "I haven't heard you play that thing in I don't know how long. You always carried that thing around and played it constantly. When your dad left you quit. You are such a beautiful singer and it was nice to hear you playing again."

"My therapist actually thought I should do something that I enjoy and this is it. Playing this guitar and singing. I forgot how much I loved to play and I missed it. I just didn't realize how much, until now."

All of a sudden my phone rings startling me and I yank it out of my bag and glancing at the caller id. "It's Will." I say surprised.

"Well answer it," my mom says with a knowing smile and walks out shutting my door to give me privacy.

"Hello?"

"Hey Tori, I wanted to make sure you got home safely. I should have called sooner actually."

"Um, yeah I did. I've been home for a while. Thanks though."

"I know that this is still really new and we aren't sure what we're doing but would you consider going out with me? We can go as a group to start out with, if you're more comfortable with that?"

I don't say anything right away. I want more than anything to go out on a one on one date but I don't feel ready to do that. It's something I have a very hard time admitting to myself.

"A group date would be a great start actually."

I hope I haven't offended him by agreeing to the group before going out with just the two of us, but I need to start out slow.

"Tori, it's okay if you're not ready. I promise. I want you to be comfortable and if it takes us having group dates from now on then that's what we'll do. Don't worry about me and my feelings. You won't hurt them, okay?"

Feeling like a weight has been lifted I reply, "Thank you Will, I really appreciate it."

With a smile in his voice he says, "No need for thanks. Just having you sitting beside me no matter who's with us is enough for me."

I smile inwardly at his words. They're sweet and sincere and in this moment I feel so very blessed.

Will then says, "I'm going to let you get to bed and I need my beauty sleep."

I chuckle at his remark and say, "Good night Will."

"Sleep tight and Tori?"

"Yes?"

"Dream of me."

Before I can respond the phone goes dead. I put it down and can't help the smile that creeps along my face. I want to dream of him and only him. I pray that I can tonight.

Some things are meant to be

Chapter 23

Tori

I had a few dreams last night and woke several times startled only to realize that I am in my bed safe and sound. I'm finally getting better at calming myself after a nightmare. Some days are worse though where I end up waking my mom or Charlie, sometimes both.

"So much for dreaming of Will," I mutter to myself.

I throw back the covers and walk to the bathroom finding Charlie in there. I stand at the doorway and say, "So um, Will called me last night with an idea."

Her eyes grow big and she smiles, turning to me and asks, "And what kind of idea did Will have?"

"He suggested a group date. What do you think?"

"Honestly? I think it's a great idea. I think you need to have some fun, which we haven't had in a really long time and plus, I think it would be good for you. Have you and Will put a 'title' on your relationship or are you just playing it by ear?"

I take a moment to think about this and finally say, "I know that we both really like each other and have deep feelings for one another. We are taking it slow to see what happens. I know I don't want to be with anybody else, for me it's Will. It's always been Will."

Charlie has a smug smile on her face and teases, "I know."

This is new to me, "What? What do you mean you know?"

She looks back at the mirror and says as if it's no big deal at all, "I may have said something to him back when Maverick and I were first dating."

With a slight tone to my voice I ask, "What did you say Charlie?"

Quickly trying to calm me she says, "I may have just told him to be patient with you and that you cared about him in your own way."

Sad isn't it that even my newly best friend at that time was completely aware of my feelings before I was able to admit them? "I'm not mad Charlie, just surprised that you knew about my feelings for him."

Turning to me and looking relieved she steps up to me and gives me a quick hug and says, "Now I am excited, squee a double date! I'm going to go and call Mav."

I roll my eyes at her choice of words and at her use of the nickname for Maverick, but can't help the chuckle and the actual glee I feel about being in a completely different setting with Will. Something I've always hoped I'd be able to do with him.

As I begin getting ready I can hear Charlie speaking animatedly on the phone with who I assume has to be Maverick. It cracks me up how excited she is. Who am I kidding? I'm so excited I just about can't think straight.

I walk to my room and finish getting ready when Charlie comes prancing in excited as hell and scaring the shit out of me in the process. "Okay, it's all set up. Sorry did I scare you? I didn't mean to."

"Yes you scared me but it's fine. What's set up to go?" I pretend to play stupid just to hear her say it.

We sit on the bed facing each other when she says, "This weekend you, me and the guys on a double date. Movie and dinner, sound good? We'll start with the 'normal' date night and then gradually escalate into doing other things." She stands there with a huge smile, so very proud of herself.

I throw my head back and laugh out loud. "You seriously crack my ass up, girl."

"What?" She asked innocently.

"Nothing, I just love how you've thought of everything and I love it."

She doesn't take offense, but smiles right on with me and says, "You know this is gonna be fun and you guys are meant to be together. I've always known that. I used to watch you pining away for him, looking when you thought no one was watching." She gets a serious look on her face all of a sudden and says, "Now I know why and I understand." She looks like she wants to say something else and then stops.

"What? Just say it. I can tell you've got something on your mind."

She looks down at her lap and I can tell she's choosing her words wisely when she says with a sad face and finally glances back up, "I just wish you thought you could have talked to me about what happened to you. For so long you were on me to tell you what was going on with me. I finally did and you know how hard that was for me and I know this is completely different but I just wish you would have felt like you could talk to me. That's all."

I don't know what to say at first and I don't get mad. Honestly she has a point, so I contemplate my response before answering. "I think I just wanted to push it so far back into the back of my mind and never remember it. How do I say this, I know it happened. I'm not naïve, I just wanted to pretend and hope that it would go away. Turns out, that's not how it works. It festers like a cancer and it eats at you until you just can't take it anymore. I wish I would have told you too so I would have dealt with this sooner rather than later, but I didn't. I'm learning that everyone deals with things differently. Unfortunately this is how I dealt with it. I can't change it, but I'm glad you're here and whether you know it or not you're a huge part of my recovery process. Having family is the best thing for me. I knew when I met you that I needed you as much as you needed me and now I know why."

She will never know how true that statement truly is. I don't realize until I've finished that I have tears running down my face and I glance over to her and to see that she's just as affected. We both wipe our eyes when we hear a throat clear. "Everything okay in here?"

Both of us start laughing when I answer, "Yes mom, we're just having a bonding moment, that's all."

She smiles and responds with, "If y'all do any more bonding you're going to turn into one person. I'm glad you have each other. You both needed each other for two very different reasons. That my girls, is what I call, meant to be."

Crab legs

Chapter 24

Tori

Tonight is the night! I'm nervous, scared and excited all at the same time. The last couple of days have crept by. Isn't that normally how it happens when you're excited about something? Will and I have spoken at school and on the phone. Not anything serious, just normal everyday things. There have been stolen looks, small conversations but nothing else. As I stand in my closet contemplating what to wear, Charlie walks in.

"I thought I was the one with the issues of figuring out what to wear?"

I smirk knowing full well that we've done a complete switch. She's dressed to kill and for once I'm completely stumped. "I don't know what my problem is."

She laughs and says, "Haha, yeah I do, you want to look perfect and I completely get that."

She reaches my closet door tapping her finger on her chin as if in complete concentration and begins to search through it. "It's gotten a lot warmer outside, why don't you wear shorts, with this?"

She holds up a sheer grass green colored top that that has lace around the back and shows some skin but you've got to wear a tank underneath it. Something I can dress up a pair of shorts with.

I throw her a knowing smile and say, "Not bad, not bad at all, your master approves, you've been taught well." I bow down to her with my hands together as if in prayer.

She smacks me lightly in the arm and says, "Turd." I can't help but laugh and walk over to my dresser and start rummaging through it looking for the perfect shorts. I pull out a pair of Bermuda shorts for her inspection and she shakes her head and says disapprovingly, "Nope."

She pushes me aside and pulls out a shorter pair of shorts in white. "These, they're perfect, and will show off those sexy long legs of yours that I've seen Will looking at for months now. Handing me the shorts, she walks back over to the closet and pulls out a pair of espadrille wedges in a shade of light brown. "Of course a pair of heels are gonna help the legs of yours get seen." I can't help but shake my head at her.

"Okay, you're the boss," I say.

She walks out of the room when I hear her mutter, "I'm sure that shit won't last long."

I laugh out loud shutting my door so I can get dressed. I feel so excited and nervous all rolled into one. I quickly dress and start on my make-up. As soon as I've finished with that, I hear a knock on the door.

The door opens and Charlie walks in, "You ready to…, wowzers girl, you are gonna have him falling all over himself."

I give her a small smile, "Hey will you help me pick out some jewelry?"

"Sure, because you know I am rocking this dressing Tori shit at the moment."

We decide on a pair of long silver earring's that have chains hanging down, a couple of bangle bracelets and silver ring with a flower on the top. I'm feeling really pretty, not going to lie, the girl did good.

All of a sudden the doorbell rings and I quickly turn to Charlie. "You look hot girl and Will is going to go nuts, just you wait until he sees you."

Her words are meant to console me, but damn I feel like a shaky mess. "Okay," I say. "Let's go."

We walk to the top of the stairs together and begin our descent down. Down at the bottom is Will and Maverick with my mom nowhere in sight. Oh my God, Will. Our eyes catch and I don't miss the look registered across his beautiful face. But it's his eyes that hold me. His brilliant green eyes capture me the whole way down and I never look away, I couldn't if I tried. I watch his eyes roam all the way down to my toes and back up. Knowing that he likes what he sees makes me happy and not uncomfortable in the least. The moment I reach him, Charlie leaves my side to go to Maverick and Will says, "You look gorgeous."

"Thank you," I breathlessly say and take a moment to look at him. He's dressed in jeans that hug every delicious curve and a button down white shirt, with his sleeves rolled up to his elbows that show off his strong, tanned arms. "You don't look too shabby yourself."

His eyes crinkle in the corners, "Thank you but you...there aren't enough words..."

I think I'm blushing and I don't blush, like ever. The feelings he elicits in me scare me a little, but I've got to say bye to mom before I go.

"Hang on, I'll be right back" I say. I walk into the other room and see my mom sitting down with a book in her lap and she looks up when she hears me.

"Are you going to be okay with this?"

"Yeah, I am. He makes me feel safe and comfortable. I don't worry or over think things when I'm with him."

She smiles and says, "Good. Have fun and call me if you need me."

I lean over and give her a quick hug, "Thanks mom." I walk back out to see them waiting for me patiently. Will puts his hand out, as if asking permission and not just taking my hand. I smile as I place it in his and follow him out the door.

We reach Maverick's car and Will opens the door for me. I smile before getting inside, finally beginning to feel somewhat like a normal girl just going on a normal date with the guy I like and my best friend.

Will gets in and we're thigh to thigh in Maverick's compact car, because of course he had to have another vintage Camaro. After he was in that horrible car accident several months back, he wanted to find one just like it, unfortunately he and his dad had restored it together. They aren't easy to come by, however they were able to find one similar in a different color. Will places his hand palm up on his leg and I turn to glance at him. He has the most intense look on his face and without turning away, I place my hand right into his. The close proximity with his hand doesn't make me cringe and has the complete opposite effect on me. It's a simple touch of feeling safe and cherished. He leans down and drops his forehead onto mine. I close my eyes at the contact and breathe him in. He smells of mint and a light cologne and of Will; my Will.

The fact that I just called him 'my' Will, in my head doesn't escape me. In this very moment and what I hope will become permanent is that he will become my Will; one day.

He straightens back up, looking directly at me and says, "God, I have waited for this for so long. You completely take my breath away."

I have nothing to say, how do I top that that? I'm such a dumb ass, all I say is, "Me too."

"Shit Tori, you are an idiot and you need to work on your vocabulary," I berate myself, completely in my head, of course.

He smiles and thinks nothing of it.

We reach our destination and I look around. Yeah a seafood restaurant! "Yes, I love me some seafood," I say.

Charlie, Maverick and Will all chuckle and Charlie says, "Yes we know Tori. There was never a question of where we'd be eating."

Will pipes up and says, "Yeah, I've never seen a girl eat shrimp like you do." He then leans into my ear and whispers, "I'm actually hoping to watch you eat crab legs."

Lord. Have. Mercy! That voice in my ear causes shivers to spike and traipse down my spine.

Okay, so I'm easily sold with seafood. Not just that but he knew what I'd want to eat and he's willing to watch me lick my fingers while eating crab legs, which is messy. All of a sudden it dawns on me.

Ooooohhhhh, I get it now and I think I'm blushing again. What the hell is wrong with me? I don't blush!

Before I can respond he gets out holding the door open for me, his hand reaching out for me to take, which is quickly becoming a very natural thing for me to do. I grab it without hesitation and let him guide me through the restaurant following on the heels of Maverick and Charlie. They sit us down in a booth and he never lets go of my hand. I could get used to this very easily. I lean over and whisper, "You know I'm going to have to have my hand back when I eat, right?"

Turning to me he says quietly, "You'd better eat fast because I'm going to be needing that hand back." He has an intensity about him that tells me he isn't kidding.

I'm so dumbstruck and in awe as I say, "Okay." Then decide to push it just a tad and say back, "You know it takes time to peel crab legs, so it could be a while."

This time I receive a slight sexy as hell smirk and he replies with, "Don't you worry if I have to help you, I will."

This is an offer I can't refuse because peeling crab legs is time consuming to get to the meat. He's quickly becoming indispensable and not just in the crab department. Getting braver with my banter I say, "I may just have to keep you around then." I see his eyes darken and smolder but then I add, "You know, for seafood purposes and all." I can't help but smile after this comment.

His reaction is priceless and this time I receive a huge grin that sets me on fire everywhere. Feelings that I'm not sure if I should be feeling right at the moment; intimate feelings. I turn away, feeling ashamed for having these thoughts and glance over at Maverick and Charlie, see that they are watching us, with a smile on their faces. I feel kind of embarrassed that they just witnessed this exchange.

Charlie looks at me and winks. She doesn't even try to hide it from Will. That girl's been around me for too long. She's starting to act like me; for shame!

We finally order and chat back and forth, all four of us in a comfortable conversation. The whole time I feel Will's thumb rubbing against my hand. It's like it's not something he thinks about, a subconscious thing he just does and it feels really nice to be touched so sweetly and with care.

Our food arrives and Will glances at me with a smile, letting go of my hand.

Every so often I sense him staring at me and I catch his eyes a time or two. I do manage to eat in a timely manner all on my own, much to my disappointment. What can I say? Deep down I was kind of hoping I might need his help. Too bad I'm a pro at cracking these shells, if only I'd been a little slower.

We finish and pay the bill, and head over to the movie theater. To my utter amazement they've chosen a romantic comedy. We grab our tickets and Charlie and I make our way into the theater to grab seats while the guys grab us some popcorn and drinks. I may be full from dinner, but I am never to full for extra butter popcorn. As soon as we sit down Charlie begins to question me. "So are you okay? You look okay. Actually you look really happy."

"Slow down woman! Yes I am okay, better than okay. I'm actually very happy and I feel good, normal even. I don't feel like a freak. I feel like a normal girl that's out with her best friends and boyfriend."

Charlie smiles really big.

"Boyfriend huh?" Will says from behind me.

Oh God, if I could die. This would be the time to do it.

"I like how that sounds," He says sitting down and grabbing my hand. He leans over for my ears only and barely a breaths whisper away says, "You've always been my girl, you just needed to realize it yourself."

If he affected me before this, then that was nothing compared to how I'm feeling right now in this moment, barely able to respond I murmur, "I was, was I?"

He's so close. Close enough that if I leaned just a little closer I could kiss him. The music starts all of a sudden and the lights dim completely signaling that the movie is getting ready to start. We continue to stare at each other until there is no light left and I turn away first.

My heart beats a million miles a minute and questions bobble around in my head. If I'd kissed him would I have flipped out on him causing a commotion in the theater? I'm not sure if I'm ready for that or for this. But I can't deny that the physical contact of hand holding has been completely fine. I haven't shied away from his touch so far. I remind myself that there are no expectations and he himself even said that he was fine with slow or whatever pace I'm willing to go. He respects it; respects me.

I am completely aware of him and he makes a point of reminding me with his back and forth thumb motion on my hand. I find it hard to concentrate on the movie with him so close, the smell of his cologne, his hand and just his overall nearness. Charlie nudges me and catching my eye and mouths, "Are you okay?"

I give her a slight nod and mouth a yes. How do I explain it? I am fine, but I just want to be a normal girl with a boyfriend. I want to be a girl that doesn't have to over think her feelings for her guy. A girl that doesn't have to be concerned with whether or not kissing her boyfriend would set her off and go crazy. I spend the rest of the movie over thinking everything.

Walking to the car Will gently tugs on my hand, "You're quiet, anything that you want to talk about? I hope I haven't done anything to make you feel uncomfortable."

I quickly respond back with, "No Will, you've been perfect. It's not you at all."

"Are you sure? Because you know I'll listen."

"Hey Maverick," he hollers. "We're going to go for a quick walk. Meet you in a few minutes." Will pulls me away and we go out on our own. We start to walk down the street, stopping at a bench in the square before asking, "What's on your mind and what are you worrying yourself about?"

I'm completely surprised at how attuned he is to me and my moods. I take a deep breath and put it out there, "I wanted to kiss you in the theater."

"I know, but not as much as I wanted to kiss you," he says. "However, you aren't ready for that and I need you to be ready before we kiss again. I want you to be one hundred percent sure when we do, without any question. Because when I kiss you, I want you to feel everything with me in the moment. No second guessing in your head."

Don't ask me why I ask this, but in a very Tori like fashion I ask, "Why do you like me so much and why have you waited so long for me?"

Without any hesitation he answers, "The first time I saw you, that hair of yours grabbed my attention. It was the prettiest shade of red that I'd ever seen. But I noticed this beautiful face and I may have noticed your long legs," he says with a shameful laugh. "What really got me was how outspoken and outgoing you were. You treated people with respect and you didn't act like your shit don't stink."

I'm completely surprised at his open admission when I blurt out, "I love you Will."

I feel embarrassed and I turn my head away. I did not mean to just throw that out.

Taking his hand and gently turning my head to face him so we are eye level he tenderly says, "I love you Tori and I've hoped and waited for so long to hear you say those words to me." He cups my face with his hands and strokes my cheeks with the pads of his thumbs.

There aren't enough words to describe how I'm feeling right now. I'm elated and happy but more than anything, I am grateful. I am grateful that this perfect guy is mine.

He leans over and kisses my forehead and I close my eyes at the contact and my breath hitches when he suddenly leans back and says, "Come on let's get you ladies home."

I almost whimper at the loss of contact until he instantly grabs my hand back, making me feel a little better.

We reach the car and see Maverick and Charlie kissing. Will clears his throat and they jump apart quickly, startled. Charlie looks embarrassed, but Maverick just throws his arms around her shoulder and smiles unabashedly chuckling softly. "What can I say? I love kissing my girl."

She lightly smacks his arm and he opens the door for her. We get in and drive home. Will's arm wraps around my shoulders and I snuggle in next to him, his other hand holding mine.

The guys walk us to the door and Will leans over kissing my forehead once again and says, "Goodnight Tori, dream of me."

As I walk into the house I think to myself. Maybe, just maybe, I might.

Guilt will eat at you

Chapter 25

Will

Maverick and I drive in silence to his house so I can pick up my truck. As I get out he asks me, "What's going on with you? Everything looks like it went well tonight, so what's up? Talk."

It did go well; better than well, it was perfect. She loves me and I love her and I love everything about her, but I'm still feeling guilty. I choose my words carefully when I say, "I'm feeling guilty because I haven't told her that I saw her that night. I feel like I should, but I'm scared that I'll lose her all over again."

Maverick looks at me thoughtfully before replying, "I agree that there shouldn't be any secrets between you. If you feel guilty over that, then you need to tell her. If you don't, it'll eat at you until it screws up your relationship and I know you don't want that."

I know he's right but I'm scared about the repercussions that this conversation could lead to. "Yeah, I know," I sigh.

I tell him goodbye and head for home and decide to focus on the positive. After everything she's been through, she still told me she loves me. Those three words mean everything to me.

I think about the entire date. When she walked down those stairs, Lord have mercy she was gorgeous and getting to hold her hand practically all night was a bonus. I had to keep telling myself to go slow. At the theater I knew she wanted to kiss me, but holy hell it took a huge ass amount of resistance to not do the one thing I so desperately wanted to do. I know she needs time and I'm not going to rush her but it was so hard keeping my lips to myself. I knew she was affected by me as much as I was by her.

I make it home safely and walk up to my room and decide to call her. Laying on the bed, I yank out my phone and scroll down and push the button.

"Hey Will," I can hear the smile in her voice.

"Hey baby, I just wanted to make sure you had a nice time tonight."

"I had a really good time Will, thank you for tonight," she says in her sexy voice.

Just the sound of her voice does so many things to me. "Well, I'm glad you had fun."

"Hey Will, can I ask you something?"

"Of course, you can ask me anything."

She hesitates for just a moment before asking, "Next time, can we go out, just the two of us? I mean I love going out with Maverick and Charlie, but I'd really like to try a one on one date with just the two of us."

"Are you sure?" I ask. I would love nothing more but I need to make sure she's really fine with this first. It would kill me if it made her uncomfortable in any way.

"I am," she replies. "I need to do this for me. I need to feel like a normal couple."

I sigh happily and say, "I love that you call us a couple."

She lightly laughs on the phone, "Do you now?"

"Oh yeah, more than you know. How does next Friday sound?"

"It sounds perfect."

"Hey Tori, do you trust me? I know this is an odd question, but I need you to know that I would never do anything to hurt you?"

Just a moment goes by before she responds, "I do. I really, truly do."

I breathe out a sigh of relief, hoping that this confirmation is enough and that when I do need to tell her that she'll take it all right.

"Good and Tori, I love you, sleep well."

"I love you too Will. Night."

It makes me feel like I'm ten feet tall hearing her tell me those words. We hang up and I lay there for several minutes feeling hopeful. My fiery redhead is finally coming back and the best part is, she's mine.

The bitches are back

Chapter 26

Tori

The rest of the weekend flies by and it's Monday morning before I know it. Today after school is another group session but I get to see Will today. We've talked several times throughout the weekend, but seeing him in person is different. I'm excited to see him this morning and curious how we'll be together in school. I carefully choose my clothes and get dressed, feeling a little giddy about seeing him. I'm beginning to slowly but surely feel more like me. There aren't any pretenses with Will. He knows everything and there aren't any secrets between us.

I hurriedly get ready and meet Charlie in the kitchen. She glances up and then looks at the clock on the microwave. "You're not ready to get to school are you?" She gives me a knowing smile.

"Maybe," I can't help the smile that takes over my whole entire face.

Charlie laughs, "You're glowing T, I love seeing you so happy."

"I am happy and I'm dealing with it in the best way that I can. I mean I can't think of one thing without the other. They go together but they don't, does that make sense?"

"I think so," she replies.

I take a moment to try to explain this better. "It's like this, every decision I make with Will is going to lead me back to that night. Being raped has affected me having a relationship with anyone, no matter who it is. For instance I wanted to kiss him the other night, but I didn't feel like I was ready because I was afraid of freaking out on him. Hence, it goes back to that night. I can't do anything about that, but with help and hearing other's experiences, it's getting a little easier."

Looking a little sad she says, "I understand what you're saying T. I'm just so sorry that you ever went through this and this happened to you."

I glance away for a moment before replying, trying to contain my emotions and look back at her. "You know what, no one deserves this but if there's one thing that I've learned through all of this is that I'm stronger than I ever gave myself credit for. If I can get through this then I can get through anything. I honestly believe that." I walk over to her and throw my arm around her. "I couldn't have done it without you and mom. You know I love you Char."

She gives me a little squeeze. "Okay enough of this mushy stuff, we'd better get to school before we're late. I know you want to see Will before school starts."

Not wanting to hide my feelings for him any longer, "You know I do." I wink as I walk out the door. "Meet you there."

The closer I get to school, the more evident the butterflies in my stomach become. I park right next to Charlie and see her looking straight ahead. I follow her eyesight and I see the guys leaning together on Maverick's car. Trying to maintain my excitement, I attempt to play it cool. I get out, grabbing my bag and slinging it over my shoulder and wait for Charlie. We walk over to them together, of course Maverick's eyes are only for Charlie, but he quickly glances over acknowledging me. I say hi and then glance at Will, whose eyes are following my entire walk over to him. I'm getting braver so I give him my trademark smile and say, "Hey there handsome." He smiles big and the moment I reach him, he grabs my hand and pulls me lightly towards him and whispers in my ear, causing shivers to race down my back.

"Hey gorgeous, I've missed you."

"We just talked last night," I tell him. I know what he means though, it isn't the same. I've missed him as well.

"Not the same as being right next you, or touching you." He pulls my hand up so it's between us.

Breathlessly I say, "No it's not."

He leans over and kisses my forehead.

This kissing the forehead thing is going to get old really fast if I don't get my shit together. It's sweet, but damn Gina, I ache for a normal kiss. I give myself an inner pep talk, telling myself that I don't know if I'm ready for that yet and I need to give myself a break.

All of a sudden I hear the most obnoxious girls' voices.

"Hey Will," they say in unison.

Ugh 'the bitches', Ashley and Miranda.

Will barely glances at them giving them a slight nod but never looks at them.

I know for a fact that he's not crazy about these two, they're freaking leaches and they made Charlie's life hell when she and Maverick had broken up. I can't resist being a bitch back so I turn around and look them straight in the eye and say, "Have you met my boyfriend?"

I pull away slightly from Will and show them our hand holding. I get a couple of glares back. "Later ladies," I say and turn back to Will who has a smile/smirk across his face.

"What?" I ask laughing.

"That was awesome and so damn hot. I love you being possessive of me and I especially love you calling me your boyfriend."

Okay maybe I was a little possessive but I wanted them to know that he was taken and to walk away. "They're bitches Will, you know that. They just needed to know that you are taken and mine."

His eyes darken at the word mine. He pulls me closer and growls, "It's getting harder and harder for me not to kiss you… But I am a very patient guy and you are so worth waiting for."

I pull his hand to my mouth kissing the top of it. "Will this do for now?"

He smiles nodding but looking affected by a simple kiss on the hand. Clearing his throat he says, "Come on woman, we've got a month left of school, let's get this day done."

There is nothing like walking hand in hand into school with him. Nothing. Now I know what Charlie was feeling when she walked in with Maverick for the very first time.

We spend the day in between classes' hand holding and quietly talking to each other. I can feel prying eyes all around us throughout the entire day. Some completely taken by surprised that we're a couple, I'm not sure why, the four of us are always together anyway. I spot 'the bitches' several times giving me eat shit looks. I just smile sweetly, because that's how I roll.

At the end of the day we walk out together to our respective vehicles. We stop at mine and he leans over kissing my forehead once again. "Call me tonight when you get home and let me know you got home safe?"

"Of course."

I squeeze his hand when I hear the most annoying voice. "You know Will, if you need a little something, something that she's not providing, you know where to find me."

Will glances her way and looks irritated with her. "Not if you were the last girl on the planet Ashley."

I don't respond to her but I'm a little shaken. It all boils back to sex and my doubts begin to pile up.

He tilts my head up making sure that we're in direct eye contact and says, "Hey, ignore her. Okay? She is nothing and says stupid shit, you know that."

I nod my head, opening my car door and getting in. Before he shuts it he says quietly, "Love you and call me."

He doesn't wait for me to answer before shutting the door. I wave and pull out, heading for group.

This is a part of the relationship that hangs over my head like a proverbial monsoon. Is this something he'll be able to handle? This is where I am completely insecure. Am I going to be enough for him? I know he's not that kind of guy, but that's the thing, he's a guy. I know they have their needs.

I reach the church where group is held and walk through those doors. It seems like it's been a long time since I first made myself walk through the threshold. Hard to believe it's only been a week. I walk through feeling so much more comfortable after last week's session. I think having a bunch of females discuss their most private and demeaning moments will thrust you into it front and center, making you deal with it. If these people that don't know me can share then why shouldn't I? Don't get me wrong, I'm scared out of my damn mind. My heart is beating faster than normal due to my nervousness, but I press on.

I spot Tiffiney and Sam and gingerly walk over to them to say hello. The moment I reach them, Sam smiles and says, "Hi Tori, right?"

"Yes, and you're Sam and Tiffiney?" I say looking directly at each one to make sure I've got it right. Hell, it wouldn't be the first time I got two people's names incorrect.

They nod and looking at Tiffiney I ask, "Can I ask you a question?"

"Sure, I'm pretty open. But I think I know what you're going to ask, this is a question about my boyfriend, right?"

I feel slightly embarrassed about this question, but decide to ask anyway, "I know you said that your boyfriend has been very supportive but how hard was it to kiss him for the first time?"

Noticing my discomfort she answers, "Don't feel embarrassed, it's a valid question. I think it's different for everyone. Cameron's been very supportive and I had to learn to feel comfortable to be around a male again. I mean, deep down I knew he wouldn't hurt me, but it was instinct to move away at the very beginning. I almost had to train and tell myself that it was okay and that he'd never hurt me. I spent so much time with him and he didn't want to leave my side, but he respected my space. Not to say that it was easy. It wasn't and it was harder than anything for him to try to get past his anger with it. He's still working on it. As far as kissing goes, it wasn't too long, but don't rush it. Do it when you feel ready. It's different for everybody."

I'm amazed at how open and understanding she is with all of my questions. "Thank you for being so open with me." I feel the need to share seeing as how she was understanding with my questions. "I told Will and he did get angry but not at me. He's been very patient and still wants to be with me, which I completely find surreal."

We walk over to our seats and get ready for group to start. Tiffiney says, "Well, you and I are the lucky ones, most of the time your first instinct is correct as far as being open about your rape with your boyfriend. Most guys don't stick around, so we're lucky, it doesn't happen often."

I nod my head in agreement and group begins. We discuss openly about certain feelings and steps we'd taken after we'd been raped. It amazes me that I'm not the only one that tried to forget it and pretend that it never happened.

I decide to share some of my story. Looking down at my hands I say, "I walked home as soon as it happened in a daze and got in the shower and scrubbed myself clean. That was my first instinct. I thought I could scrub it all away. Obviously you can't and I didn't. But my first instinct was not to go the police." I glance back up, looking around me at all of these people that have been through this and feel a sense of companionship and closeness with perfect strangers. The things that have been discussed are so personal and I feel so much more at ease this time around. "I've never told anyone that before."

The instructor smiles at me, "Thank you for sharing that with us Tori. Many don't go the police right after it's happened. Yes, you should but a lot of times that isn't your first instinct. Everyone is different and no matter what anyone says there is no right or wrong way. I can't tell you that going home to wash yourself clean was bad. This I can tell you without a doubt. You're here and you're getting help. You are no longer a victim, but a survivor, taking the necessary steps to heal yourself and that you should be commended for. You all should."

I smile inwardly knowing that I'm doing everything I can to help me and it feels pretty damn good.

Normal is highly overrated

Chapter 27

Tori

I lay on top of my bed and contemplate the last several days. I had my therapy appointment, where I discussed in detail mind you, several things that were far from pleasant to talk about and it put me in a funk for a couple of days. I had to go into detail about my rape. I'd been avoiding it like the plague and she said we needed to revisit it, that the sooner we discussed it the better it would be for me. It was hard as hell and I broke down several times. I had to explain the 'biting kisses' that made me cringe having to repeat and the endless tears that cascaded their way down my face. We had to stop several times so I could calm down and breathe. These were things I never wanted to remember and things that I hadn't told anyone, including my mom or Charlie. It's hard to relive the past when you want so very desperately to forget it.

Towards the end of the session she brought up Will and wanted to know where we stood and how I was feeling. I talked about our group date and how it went and how I had told him that I'd loved him, but that I hadn't meant to, it had just sort of slipped out. To my surprise she said that it wasn't a bad thing. It meant that I was letting my actual feelings for him take over and I wasn't living in the past, seeing myself as unworthy of being loved. She said that it was a good sign and that it meant I was beginning to heal. She also reiterated that I would go through moments of second guessing myself, which I know I have. I've done it repeatedly already, over and over.

I asked her what she thought about my one on one date with Will. Given it had been my idea she didn't see a problem with it as long as I felt comfortable and I was taking a positive step. I ended the conversation telling her that I just wanted to be normal and be able to kiss Will without feeling scared that I would freak out. She'd told me that being normal was highly overrated. I thought it was a funny thing for a therapist to say.

Will's been great but I'm concerned that something is bothering him. At first I thought that he might be having second thoughts about me or us, but his actions don't support that. I can't quite put my finger on it. He's attentive and caring and always mindful of my feelings. Constantly, he makes a point of hand holding, always needing to touch me.

My forehead also seems to be getting a lot of action these days and my lips are starting to get jealous. My mind goes back and forth with, "Am I ready for this or am I going to flip out?" Dr. Heart thinks that I'm over-thinking it and says I need to just take things slow and listen to my instincts. I know she's right, but hell, I'm human and I can't help it. I over-think things now and I never used to. I never would have spent so much time on the thought of kissing Will, I would have just done it. But rape will change you in several different ways. In some ways I'm still the old Tori but in a lot of ways I'm not. This Tori has some insecurities now that I didn't have before. This Tori thinks things through when before I would have jumped without ever giving it a second thought.

I've had to ward 'the bitches' off a couple of times. Maverick and Will have both told them to back off several times but they don't seem to get it. Charlie and I have taken it upon ourselves several times to tell them to back the hell off. Charlie's been very vocal, which normally isn't her, it is some seriously funny shit. Maverick and Will just stand there with smiles on their faces, like they're enjoying the show, watching their girls get territorial. Guys can be such turds. Though I've never seen such desperate girls who didn't understand the concept of no. I almost feel sorry for them; almost.

So many things run through my mind. Tomorrow is my one on one date with Will. I'm excited about it being the two of us but I'm also nervous and I don't want to screw anything up. I decide to quit thinking so damn much and hop up off of the bed and pick out my clothes for tomorrow. I'm not sure why, but this time it's easier to dress myself. I decide on a cute eyelet summer dress. It's fitted and a little on the short side, showcasing my tan legs and small waist. I hang it up at the top of the frame of my closet when I hear a knock on the door.

"Come in."

My mom peeps her head in the door and walks in. "Do you have a few minutes to talk?"

"Sure, what's up?"

She looks down and I can tell that she's thinking long and hard before she says whatever's on her mind. "I've been doing a lot of thinking and I do mean a lot."

"Okay," I say tentatively.

She pats the side of the bed, signaling for me to take a seat next to her and sighs, looking up at me. "I want you and me to go the police." Before I can respond she holds up her hand signaling that's she's not done. "I know it's been a year since your rape, but Tori, I feel like we need to go talk to them and at least give your best description that you can. I made a call and spoke to a detective. He was really nice and not what I expected, he seemed genuinely concerned and said that coming in now would still be okay. That there is still a possibility that your description could be similar to someone else's. Let's face it honey, if this happened to you then chances are it has happened to someone else." She rushes on, "I haven't wanted to push you and you've been doing so well the last couple of weeks, but Tori it's time. I know you're still having nightmares, but I think this could help them. It pisses me off that this guy is running loose and who knows we may be able to find the ass hole."

"You're right," heaving out a breath of air. She looks as if she's getting ready to argue with me, but then at hearing my words, looks relieved.

"Really? You're not going to fight with me?"

I shake my head no. "How can I argue with that? I need to do something and maybe this will make me feel like I'm doing it. Truthfully I should have gone a year ago, instead I've ended up holding onto it for a year and never told a soul. Again, I should have gone a couple of weeks ago but I was a mess. These last couple of weeks have taught me so much. Don't get me wrong I'm messed up still, without a doubt, but if I can do something, anything to make this right, I will. I'm just now realizing my strength and finally beginning to heal."

With tears in her eyes, she grabs my hand. "I'm so, so proud of you and I'm so very proud to call you my daughter."

I lean my head down on her shoulder and a couple of tears trickle down. "I really wish I'd told you when it first happened. I was just so ashamed and felt so guilty. I felt for the longest time that it was my fault and I never wanted to disappoint you. I know it isn't, but some days I have to remind myself of that."

"Tori, don't you realize that you could never disappoint me? I love you so much and if you ever need reminding on those bad days, come find me. It may not help, but I will always be here to remind you that you were innocent and blameless in your rape."

I don't say anything at first and we sit in silence for a few more minutes. Finally I say, "I told Will I loved him last week. I didn't mean to, but I blurted it out. I've liked him for so long but it was solidified the day I took a chance and told him my deepest and darkest secret. He didn't treat me any different and treated me like I was special even though…"

I trail off because I hate saying it, the words been said enough tonight.

"I know, I can tell," my mom says, "He's a good guy. I've always liked Will and I knew you both liked each other and I could see it grow into more, but then talks of Will disappeared. I will always feel some sort of guilt for not asking about it. I should have realized something had happened and that your behavior had changed. You did a good job of hiding it and acting like everything was okay, but I'm your mother and I should have known. I was still consumed with missing your dad I think and I'll never forgive myself for that."

I lean up and look at her and can't believe that she feels guilty over this. "No mom, don't feel guilty. You were still going through things. I know you tried to hide it, but I knew you were."

"Well Tori, it's my job as your mom to know when something isn't right and I'm sorry, I truly am."

"Well I think it's time we both quit feeling guilty over things that happened in the past that we have no control over, don't you think?" I say looking up to her.

"How did you get so smart? Oh yeah, because you take after me."

Yep the apple didn't fall far from the tree, that's where I get my smart mouth from.

My mom looks over at the dress hanging over the closet door. "Is that what you're wearing tomorrow on your date?"

"Yep, you like?"

"That Will is some lucky guy," She says and winks at me. "Are you sure you're fine to go out tomorrow night with just the two of you?"

I nod my head yes and reply, "I feel comfortable with him. He treats me with such care, sometimes too much care." I grumble the last part quietly and look away a little embarrassed at my statement. I sigh and say, "I'm appreciative and grateful of how he treats me, but my head is getting a ton of action lately."

My mom throws her head back and laughs, "I for one am glad he's this way."

"Yeah, I know me too. I want to see if I can handle kissing him without freaking. I'm just talking about a kiss, not a complete make out session."

Just then my cell phone rings. I get up to grab it and look down at the screen. "It's Will."

"Yeah, I can tell, because you have this massive grin plastered across your face. Thank you for the talk. You and I will be making a trip tomorrow, the moment you get out of school, before your date. And Tori, I love you."

"Love you too mom."

I quickly answer the phone before the ringing quits. "Hello?"

"Hey baby," Will says.

"Hey," I reply sounding rather shy.

"I was thinking about our date tomorrow. How do you feel about going to the diner and then to the lake for a little night swimming? I wanted to make sure you were comfortable with it first before we do it."

"Yeah, that sounds fine but I have to go somewhere with my mom as soon as I get home from school." I don't know what his reaction is going to be so I nervously take a deep breath and say, "I'm going with my mom to fill out a police report."

There's silence at first, but then Will whooshes out a breath and says, "I'm so glad that you're doing this."

I feel utter relief, "My mom talked to me about tonight and I'm ready to do this. I can't guarantee what kind of mood I'll be in afterwards but I can't put it off any longer, regardless of the outcome."

"No, I agree with your mom. It's important and you never know what information could help." He's quiet for a moment before asking, "Would you be okay with rescheduling our date for Saturday instead?" He quickly continues, "This isn't going to be any easy thing to do and I just think going out right afterwards probably isn't the best idea."

I'm sad to postpone but he's right, I need to do this and I'd be lying if I said that I wouldn't be affected by it. "Yeah, that'd be okay. You're probably right."

"How about this, if you feel up to it afterwards and you need me, call me and I'll be there if your mom's cool with it. Call me anyway, but if you want me there, I'll be there."

I love how thoughtful he is, but I don't know if I want him to see me like that again; crying and out of control. "I'll call you afterwards and let you know. Deal?"

"Sure," he replies softly.

We talk for several minutes about mundane things before we hang up and he tells me, "Tori, I really am so proud of you."

My heart swells at this and it makes me love him all the more. "Thank you."

We get off the phone and I crawl into the covers with my thoughts solely on Will and my pit stop at the police station. I'm not nervous yet but I know I will be.

I fall asleep with thoughts of Will and only Will and his penetrating green eyes that see me for me.

Dick head

Chapter 28

I get off the phone with Tori and know I have a huge goofy ass smile slapped across my face. God, I love hearing her voice on the phone. That husky voice of hers sets me on fire and I still can't believe that she's all mine. Every part of her is completely perfect in my eyes.

I'm so damned proud of her for taking the step to go to the police. I know this is such a difficult and hard thing for her, but the fact that she's doing it speaks volumes of her.

My mind trails off and I think about what I've been up to. I don't like hiding things from Tori but I don't want her to worry. In a way I feel like I'm not being completely honest with her. I sigh, I know I'm not. Between having to tell her that I'd seen her in that damn truck and left, and that Maverick and I were doing our own detective work, I'm really not batting a thousand. Maverick and I have been taking steps to figuring out who that dick head was at that party over a year ago. We'd cornered Ty this week at school who said he couldn't remember. "It had been too long ago, he'd said." I had walked off in a pissy mood, feeling like this was going to be an impossible task. Of course Ty had wanted to know why. I'd left after that question.

Maverick told Ty thanks and followed me, telling me not to worry, that we'd find the guy. I know if the roles were reversed I'd be the level headed one. He suggested we check with some of the other guys from the party. The thought calmed me a bit and I got mad at myself for getting upset so easily. I have to remember that there are others to ask. Someone had to know who he was. Someone had invited that sack of shit, he hadn't just shown up on his own.

I try to shake the fucker out of my head and focus on Tori. I've never felt for anybody like I do for Tori and aim to make sure that she has the best time Saturday. I want it to be perfect. I need to give her the perfect date, but I want it to be natural, not like I'm trying too hard. I need her to feel like we are a normal couple, something we would do at any point and time in our relationship.

I close my eyes feeling scared of the prospect of losing her after I tell her what I'd seen that night and how she's going to react. So I need the perfect date for her to remember when she's pissed as hell at me. How could she not be? I rub my hand across my face, as if I can scrub the worry away. I can't tell her Saturday night after our date. Nope, it's going to have to wait a little while longer. Saturday is about us. I'll worry about it after tomorrow night. Things will change and it's terrifying as hell.

An out of body experience

Chapter 29

Tori

I sit here on my bed, guitar in hand, strumming away to a song. I'm waiting for my mom to get home from work and trying, unsuccessfully, to calm my nerves. I can't believe I left this guitar alone for so long. I've missed it so much and I'm just now realizing it felt like a piece of my soul was missing until I picked it up again and played. I feel complete. I'm deep in concentration letting my fingers glide along the strings and quietly singing to it.

"I'm scared to death, that there may not be another one like this and I confess that I'm only holding on by a thin thin thread. I'm kicking the curb cause you never heard the word that you needed so bad."

"I love the country flair you've given it Tori. I love Adam Levine."

I jump out of my skin and fall off the bed, yet manage to hold on to my guitar the whole way down. I look up, scowling and see my mom standing there with an amused look on her face.

"Sorry honey, I really didn't mean to scare you." Of course, she says this while she's still chuckling.

"Sure mom."

I plop back on the bed, placing my guitar in my lap and continue playing.

"Are you about ready to do this? I'm sorry you had to push your date with Will to tomorrow." She walks over and sits next to me.

"No, it's okay. Not to mention he agreed with you anyway, so it's cool." I stop playing and look up at her. "Mom, I'm scared. I really am. I'm concerned about what they will say to me. What I should, or shouldn't, have done."

"We've been through this though, Tori. They won't criticize you; they just need a statement. They aren't there to judge you. The guy I talked to, Detective Harrison, was very nice when we spoke. He sounded genuinely concerned about you coming in, and glad that you weren't letting it go."

I know it's the right thing to do, I'm not discounting that. My nerves are on edge because I'll be reliving the most intimate details of my worst nightmare to a man I do not know.

Drawing on the strength I'm slowly getting back, I resolve to myself it's now, or, maybe never. "Okay, let's go, let's do it. I need to do this now." I place my guitar back in its case and grab my purse. I turn to my mom, "Lead the way."

"That's my girl."

I follow closely behind all the way to the car. My hands begin to shake and my mind wanders. There's no doubt in my mind I'm doing the right thing. I climb in the passenger seat and turn the radio on. I sing along to every song that comes on, attempting to clear my mind; attempting being the operative word.

My mom turns to me, "You'll be fine."

"Oh we're here already? Shit that was fast," I say under my breath.

Taking a deep breath, okay several deep breaths, I open the car door and meet my mom at the back of the car. She gives me an encouraging smile as I follow her inside. We walk to the counter and it's just like the ones you see in the television shows: A counter in the middle of the station with a detective standing behind it. He looks up, ignoring me, and looks directly at my mom, "Can I help you?"

Oblivious to the interested looks the policeman is giving her, Mom throws him one of her magnetic smiles and says, "Yes, we have an appointment with Detective Harrison."

Without realizing it I'm clenching my hand into a fist then unclenching. I repeat the motion over, and over, and over. We are led into another office and the door is shut with enough force to make me jump. My mom places her hand on my leg and soothes, "It's okay Tori, breathe, I'm here."

I nod my head and try desperately to slow my breathing. Clench fist, unclench fist—over and over. I finally glance at my hands and see they're turning beet red from the repetitive action. I open them once more and wipe them down my shirt.

Suddenly, the door swings open and a man, presumably the detective, walks in. He's about my mom's age and all business. He introduces himself, but when I open my mouth to introduce myself in return I only squeak. I clear my throat and try again. Second time's a charm.

Detective Harrison begins, "When your mom and I spoke on the phone, she indicated you were raped a little over a year ago."

I nod my head in confirmation.

"I'm going to need to know everything that transpired from the beginning to the very end."

I look away: Away from the detective and away from my mom. This is so, so hard. I stare at a blank ugly wall with nothing to keep my attention, but it's easier to stare than to think about what I need to do, so much easier.

"Tori," Detective Harrison says, "I know this is hard for you. It's really important that we get an accurate account of that day and the proceedings leading to your rape. I will be as gentle as I can, but I'm going to need details."

Again I nod. Words are so difficult to form.

Come on Tori you've got this. One time, that's all. Just do it and get it over with.

Trying so desperately to hold myself together, I clear my throat and begin the hardest conversation I will ever have with a stranger.

I turn and face him because this must be done face to face. He can't just see the side of my face. I need him to see and feel my pain. He won't know the horrors that were done to me from the side of my face. I begin at the beginning. I explain about my date and the drink I had for 'liquid courage'. I explain the party and how Will and I were separated, with me heading outside for fresh air. I tell him about being approached and saying no. How I was dragged away by the arm, and how it felt like my arm was being yanked out of the socket. I pause for a moment and feel my hands start to itch and burn. I rub them together trying to ease the pain. Nothing helps, nothing ever does. I return my eyes to him, steel myself and continue. "I was dragged and shoved into a pickup truck. I don't know the color, or make, or model. I know the windows were not automatic."

"How do you know for sure?"

"Because, detective, he held my hands." Unconsciously, I lift them to demonstrate the hold and continue, "He held them above my head and pressed them into the handle toward the window." Tears leak from my eyes, and I begin to rub my hands together again.

"*He* laughed while I struggled. I cried and said no so many times I lost count. *He* slapped me when I called for help, when I heard Will. I tried desperately to be heard and to be saved, but it didn't happen for me. I wasn't lucky." The tears fall, but I don't stop to wipe them dry; I let them fall.

Detective Harrison watches and listens, interrupting only a couple of times to clarify the details as he writes in his notebook. He hands me a tissue, but I just crumple it in my hands, never using it. I explain *his* term 'biting kisses' and I continue to the very end. I don't stop until I get it all out—every last gory detail. Even when *he* leaned over and opened the truck door, letting me know *he* was finally done with me, and I was dismissed. There is a flash of anger on the detective's face that I see before he can hide it. I see the anger, but more importantly, I feel it. It emanates from him in waves.

He asks if he can bring in a sketch artist. I hesitate, but only for a moment before I agree. I fidget with my hands, constantly looking at my surroundings. Detective Harrison tells me I did really well, and my mom smiles at me when she catches my eye. She looks proud of me. I look away quickly because I begin to feel shame. Not from the act itself but because I waited so long to do this, to report it instead of dealing with it.

Have you ever had an out of body experience? You're experiencing something, but at the same time you feel apart from it all; watching from above? That is how I feel right now. I see the hustle and bustle of everything around me. I see so many different kinds of people coming and going through the office window. I know my role and the importance of doing this regardless of my feelings. Has my rapist done this to others? Chances are high he has and it makes me sick to my stomach. The nausea gets so bad I stand abruptly and ask where the restroom is. Barely hearing directions I run as fast as I possibly can, afraid that I may lose the contents of my stomach before I make it. Fortunately, it's not far and I make it in time. I charge in, stumble to a stall and let go. I become aware of a hand gently holding my hair back away from my face, soothing words break though the buzzing in my ears, whispering it's okay, I'm not alone. Slowly I comprehend it's my mom soothing me, just as she's done my whole life. Crying, I continue to spill my insides into the toilet. I am horrified and ill because the sick bastard may have done to others what he did to me. Finally empty, I sit up as mom backs out of the stall, giving me room to stagger to the sink. I splash my face, and gargle water, spitting the rancid taste into the sink. Then I stand up and see my flushed face.

I turn away, searching for my mom. "I'm sorry," I sob. "I didn't mean to lose it. I know that I can do this."

"Oh honey, don't apologize, you're doing great!" Quickly closing the distance, she wraps her arms around me—cocooning me in her warm, safe embrace.

My breathing finally under control, I weakly manage, "I guess I'd better get back in there for the sketch artist."

"I know you're scared Tori and you're allowed to be. Please don't discount your feelings in all of this and make yourself feel guilty all over again. Please?"

Answering her pleading tone I say, "I know. But mom, I keep wondering if I could have saved someone this horror if only I had done this sooner. Could I have kept it from happening to someone else? I hate the thought I may have had the power to stop him. That it could be my fault if he… if he raped someone else!" I choke out with a sob.

"Tori, the system isn't perfect. Maybe you could have, maybe not, but you can't "what if" yourself sick. You have to live in the present, and continue dealing with it head on. I couldn't be more proud of you. What you did tonight is huge. You are so brave, and I know your bravery today will help someone in the future." She guides me out of the restroom and back to the detective, who is waiting with another man holding a large sketchpad.

"Are you okay, Tori?" Detective Harrison asks with genuine concern.

"Better, thank you. I'm ready to get started."

I recall every inch of my assailant's features that I possibly can. I get as detailed as possible, trying hard to remember every piece of him from that night. When we are finished the detective reassures me, "Great job, Tori, I think we have something decent here."

The sketch artist turns it around for me to see. Instantly shrinking away, my voice wobbles as I quietly confirm, "That's him." He has cruel eyes I will never forget, and a mouth in a constant sneer. It terrifies me.

"What happens now?" I'm curious about what I've accomplished tonight and how it's going to help going forward.

"Well, in the future, any other rape victims that come forward with descriptions of their assailant will be compared against the sketch of your attacker. Obviously, we can't do anything without physical evidence, but it's a good start. You also provided a very important tip this evening when you shared the term 'biting kisses' used during your attack." Wincing, he continues, "Likely, this is a term he uses with all his victims. It's a very specific phrase we can use to link the rapist to other victims. You've helped a lot tonight, whether you know it or not. You've done good kid." This time, when I meet his eyes, I receive a look of pride.

"Thanks." I say, then glance to my mom, "Take me home?"

She thanks Detective Harrison as she wraps her arms around me and guides me out of the station.

I left the police station knowing I did one of the hardest but also bravest things that I could have done. Do I wish I had done things differently a year ago? That's an easy answer, of course I do, but what's done is done, right? Maybe, just maybe, I've helped in some small way.

He's a mind reader and I'm a jackass

Chapter 30

Will

Maverick and I trudge along going from friend to friend's house trying unsuccessfully to make a connection to this guy. I'm frustrated and pissed off. "Dammit!" I holler slamming my hand on the steering wheel of my truck.

Maverick sighs, "Dude, I know, I get it. We will find this piece of shit, I swear we will. Do you want to call Tori and see how it went tonight?"

I do more than anything, but I'm concerned about overwhelming her and what if she's not finished? I'm also worried about what 'place' she'll be in, but my need to speak to her and know she's okay, surpasses all other thoughts. "Yeah, I do," I say feeling broken that I've done nothing to help her.

Before I can dial the phone, Maverick says, "You know you've already helped her a lot, right? You've done everything right to help her. You've stood by her, and while you know I would have done the same thing in your place, some guys wouldn't."

"What are you? A fucking mind reader?" I know I'm being a smart ass but I can't resist the jab.

Maverick laughs, "Um no, jackass, but I'd be feeling the same thing you're feeling right now. I can tell you feel helpless. I'm just saying I get it and you have absolutely no reason to feel this way. I swear we'll find him. Someway, somehow, we'll find him. Plus, the most important part is you have me to help, and you aren't alone," he finishes with a smirk.

"God, I hope you're right. I know it would ease Tori's mind knowing he's put away, even though I want to kill the bastard. I know she's scared he's done this to other girls. I need to do this for her, as much as for me. I feel like this is the best way I can help her."

"Bro, are you dense? You love her and pursued her despite everything and that alone is huge. You sure can be so slow sometimes," he says with a huff.

"Okay subject dropped. I'm taking your ill ass home and instead of calling, I'm going to stop by."

Maverick throws his head back and laughs, "There's the tenacious Will I know."

"Asshole," I mutter.

I drop Maverick off, thanking him for all of his help as well as putting me in my place, and drive straight to

Tori's. I feel anxious in my need to get to her as quickly as possible, trying my best to obey the speed limit 'cause hell I'm no good to her if I'm stopped, or worse killed, on the way. I finally pull into her driveway, quickly jog up the steps and ring the doorbell.

Charlie answers and invites me in. "How is she?" I ask before I'm even completely in the house.

She whispers, "I wasn't there but Shelby told me about it. It was rough, but she did it and she did a great job. She was really strong and handled herself rather well. She had a moment that she had to leave, but she went right back in. She'll be glad you're here. Come on, she's in the living room."

I follow Charlie further into the house; my need to see Tori and prove to myself she's okay is overpowering everything I was feeling just twenty minutes earlier. She's laying on the couch with the television on. Since she doesn't hear me enter, I take a moment and take in everything that is Tori. Her magnificent hair is splayed across the sofa pillow and she has a blanket thrown over her. I walk over to her, "Hey baby."

She turns and our eyes catch when she sees me. She smiles and starts to get up. "No, stay right there." I sit down on the floor in front of the couch and she gives me her hand.

"What are you doing here?"

"I needed to know my girl was okay. I was worried about you." I hold her hand and rub my thumb across her knuckles, loving the feeling of touching her.

Her eyes sparkle and she smiles a small smile, "I'm so glad you did. But I am fine. I did what I had to do, what needed to be done. What I should have done earlier."

"No baby, you did it when you were ready and that's what matters." She doesn't say anything, just stares at me.

"I'm glad you're here," she whispers.

"Yeah, me too."

"What did you do tonight?"

Her question catches me off guard, it wasn't one I was prepared for. "Oh, me and Maverick hung out and I just dropped him off."

She accepts my answer without a second thought. I don't like keeping this from her, but it's something that I can't tell her, not yet. All of sudden I feel like such an asshole for keeping things from her. From seeing her in that damn truck to this, I'm such a fucktard.

"Will you lay with me and hold me?" She looks away for a second before looking at me directly in the eye. "I need you to hold me. I need that closeness with you. Something that is pure and innocent from someone who loves me." A single tear falls from her eye and without a second thought I reach forward and smooth it away.

"You don't have to ask twice." I crawl behind her, pulling her to me and wrapping my arms around her. She snuggles into my arms and it feels like home. She feels like home, this is where she is meant to be. Her hair tickles my nose but it's nice and smells like strawberries. It's still hard for me to wrap my head around that she's mine. We lay there for several minutes before I hear her breathing even out and I realize she's fallen asleep in my arms. Shelby walks in a few minutes later, smiling when she spots us.

"She finally fell asleep huh? I'm glad. She did good tonight, she really did." She continues to tell me quietly how it all went and how strong my girl is, which I have never doubted for an instant. Shelby finishes and starts to walk out before stopping, turning around and telling me I can stay the night, if I want to. "I trust you Will and I'm grateful she has you in her life."

"Thank you, that means a lot," then I shake my head and say, "But no, I'm the grateful one," I say with all the sincerity I can muster. She nods her head and walks out.

Holding her in my arms is indescribable. I look down at Tori and my heart swells for this brave beautiful girl in my arms and if it's at all possible, I love her even more.

Frozen

Chapter 31

Tori

I wake up and my first thought is I didn't have a nightmare, but my second thought is I'm not in my bed, and someone's strong and rather heavy arm is thrown around me, tucking me into his chest protectively. I sit up with a start as the thought fully forms in my head. My heart racing, I turn and see Will sleeping soundly. I watch him sleep as my heart begins to slow. Even in sleep he's as handsome as ever. His perfect lips look so damn kissable and I can't quit staring. A lock of his dirty blond hair is hanging over his eye and without thinking, my hand moves to sweep it away. It's soft between my fingers and I linger longer than I really should, but I it feels nice. I notice a slight frown line between his eyes. I slide fingers to it attempt to lightly rub it away. After staring at him longer than I really should, and feeling like a complete dork, I decide to snuggle back into his arms. It was nice and safe before my mini freak-out. As I begin to lie back down, I hear,

"I wondered when you were going to lie back down with me." I jump a little, startled, and a smile tugs at the corner of his mouth.

"You ass! How long have you been awake?" I can't stop the grin that creeps across my face.

"Since you first jumped up, which I realize you probably did because you didn't expect me to still be here." He frowns, "I'm sorry I scared you."

"No, it's my fault. It just surprised me." I immediately remember he's now seeing me first thing in the morning. I instantly begin to comb my fingers through my hair trying to smooth my bed head down.

"You look beautiful, Tori."

I tilt my head to the side asking, "How did you know?"

He doesn't hesitate. "It was written across your face. Your expression says you just registered that you just woke up, and now I am seeing you in all your morning glory. Personally, I love this look," he says, eyes twinkling.

I lightly punch him on the arm.

"What was that for?"

"That was for pretending you were asleep the whole time, you faker."

He chuckles, "I didn't want to interrupt."

Embarrassed, I turn away.

"No, don't look away, please?" He pleads and his face loses all traces of joking. I turn back at his serious tone. "I like that you like to look at me; touching my hair and here," grabbing my fingers he guides them to the frown line I just tried to smooth away. "I love you touching me."

I lean down, see his eyes widen at my nearness, and kiss him on the forehead. It's a simple thing to someone else but Will understands it's a big thing for me. I initiated it and that is huge for me. And by the look on his face, it is for him, as well.

"Good morning," Charlie says walking in.

"Morning," We both say, never taking our eyes off one another.

"What are y'all going to do tonight?"

Will sits up on the couch but grabs my hand while turning to Charlie, "Dinner at the diner tonight and then we'll see after that." He winks at me.

Yeah, he knows exactly what he's got planned, I think to myself. I realize it doesn't scare me having Will not tell me the rest of our plans and being surprised. I trust him, especially having slept in his arms all night. I was home. I am home; with him.

He stands, kissing me on the forehead, "I'm going home to shower, and I'll be back to pick you up about 5:00? Is that okay?"

"Yes, it sounds perfect."

He smiles and kisses me again on the forehead, "Bye, baby, see you later." He turns, winks at Charlie and says goodbye.

I know I'm smiling like a fool as I watch him leave, but it can't be helped. He's just perfect.

"Now I know how you feel watching Maverick and me." Charlie says with a laugh.

I act innocent, "I don't know what you mean?"

As if she didn't hear me she says, "You weren't kidding about the forehead kissing either. He's got it bad for your forehead."

I throw my head back and laugh. I laugh until there are tears in my eyes. Charlie joins with me and takes a pillow off of the couch throwing it at me. I deflect it and throw it back at her. This is how my mom finds us ten minutes later, in a full on pillow fight with her decorative pillows.

We don't notice her right away but when we do, she stands with an enormous grin plastered on her face. "Now this—this I have missed. It's been a long time since I've seen you laugh like this."

Hearing my mom's words doesn't make me sad, not this time. "It feels really good to laugh. I feel I'm finally taking a piece of myself back. I'm finally beginning to get the old me back."

I spend most of the day helping around the house. I owe it to my mom to help; she's let me skate by without helping for a while, and I know Charlie's picked up a lot of my slack.

The day flies by and it's getting closer to Will's arrival time, and knowing him, he'll be here early. I shower and get ready as quickly as I can deciding on a halter sundress that falls a little above my knees and a pair of stacked high espadrilles. My belly is doing flip-flops from sheer excitement, and maybe a touch of nervousness. I know it'll be fine, I just need to get over being alone with a guy. But Will isn't just any guy. He is so much more than *a guy*. He is my haven, my place of safety; when I'm with him I feel protected and loved.

When the doorbell rings, I hurry downstairs to be the one to answer the door. Standing before me—I swear to all that is holy—is my Will, looking fine as ever.

Did I just use the word fine?

"Tori, you look gorgeous, as always." He takes all of me in and it's definitely not creepy. Nope, not at all. He makes me feel gorgeous.

"You're not so bad yourself," I flirt back. He has on a pair of cargos —Lord have mercy! He has nice legs— with a fitted tee that showcases his physique perfectly. The sight of him instantly sends me back to the vision of him, shirtless at the lake. Oh, yeah, he's engrained on my brain.

Grinning, "Ready?" he asks. He knows damn well I was checking him out.

The embarrassment of being caught gawking doesn't come, and I give myself a high-five. Tossing a quick goodbye to my mom, we head out to his truck. Ever the gentleman, he opens the door and lets me in before walking to his side, then grabs my hand before starting the truck. "Are you hungry?"

"Starving."

"Good," he grins and tunes the radio to a local country station. A popular, upbeat song comes on the radio. As we drive along, he steals glances at me while quietly singing along to *I Got You* by Thompson Square, beaming the whole time.

I got you the missing piece that makes me feel. I got you the breath I breathe and there ain't nothing else I need.

It's sweet and romantic, and if I'm not mistaken he's singing the song to *me*. He's not the best singer but it doesn't matter, the words say enough. When the song ends we chat for a few minutes before arriving at the diner. This isn't just *any* diner. This place has the very best burgers and homemade french fries you've ever tasted.

We park, and after Will opens my door, we stroll inside, hand in hand. I love the feeling of his hand in mine and knowing everyone knows we're together. As soon as we clear the doorway, I inwardly groan and whisper in Will's ear, "Don't look now but that bitch Ashley is here."

"Too late," he says. "It looks like she's waiting for someone, because we both know she'd never be eating by herself."

"Okay, you're right. Please be right," I nervously chuckle. The last thing I need is Ashley ruining my date with Will. She spots us and with a mischievous look in her eyes, she throws a small, smartass wave. Yes, waves can be smartass, trust me.

We're led to our table and I'm relieved Ashley's table is well behind us and my back is to her. Will immediately captures my hand as our waitress walks up. I'm not blind; her ogling is very obvious, but I don't care.

Let her look like an idiot.

We place our orders and ease into conversation that's nice, and simple. Simple in such a very good way: I can be me because I know it's good enough for him.

Our food comes and I devour it like I haven't eaten all day. I forget all about Ashley until I hear the most obnoxious, loud laughter that can only belong to her. Apparently, her date finally showed up, no way she'd be laughing like that by her lonesome. I attempt to ignore it, but damn, it's like she's trying too hard to be noticed.

Another laugh suddenly cuts through Ashley's. It's eerily familiar. Goose bumps rise across my entire body and the hair at the nape of my neck stands up. I notice my hands are shaking and that I'm breathing heavily. I'm frozen in fear. Something about that laugh reminds me of my nightmares. I faintly hear Will calling my name, but it doesn't register. Even though he's sitting right across from me I can't see him. I'm rooted to the spot, unable to move. But I have to. I can't sit here. I have to move, I have to get away. I force my body to stand up, cursing my feet to move the fuck on. I have to get out of here, I have to. I vaguely notice someone helping me out of the diner. I don't fight it because I'm moving away from the laugh, not towards it. I'm guided to a truck, Will's truck, and I'm helped inside. I start rocking back and forth, back and forth. My hands and palms are aching and itching and I claw at them, over and over.

Will's voice finally breaks through the storm in my head, "Baby, what is it, what can I do?"

Miraculously I choke out, "Home."

I only notice the forward movement of the truck, oblivious to anything and everything around me. Finally, the movement stops and I'm floating as Will's strong arms carry me away. Distantly, a voice calls for Shelby and more voices are suddenly surrounding me. I don't understand anything, it's just noise. The floating stops and the strong arms cradle me, rocking me, soothing me. Calming sounds edge their way in and begin to overtake the laugh, but I still hear it. I hear the laugh. Briefly, awareness resumes as soft fingers wipe wetness from my face. And then, sleep overtakes me.

Brave new girl

Chapter 32

Tori

For the second day in a row I wake up in Will's arms, but this time I'm not smiling. No, this time I wake with fear, not from being in Will's arms, but from the laugh. I know that laugh and it is one I hoped to never hear again. The owner of that laugh took something from me. When I begin to move, Will's eyes flutter open.

"Tori, are you okay? I was so worried and I didn't know what to do."

I'm horrified our date was ruined, but I won't blame this on me, not this time. The person that owns that laugh ruined it. "I'm sorry about last night."

He begins to shush me, "Shush, baby they're will be others."

He's always so understanding and my stomach clenches at what I need to say to him, to all of them.

213

Just when I'm finally getting myself put back together, I feel the pieces begin to unravel once again. I take note that my mom is asleep in the recliner and that Charlie is on the floor on a handmade pallet. I'm not alone and I can do this. Everyone I love is in this room.

"I have… I have to tell you something."

He looks at me with compassion and understanding and just nods his head, "Okay."

"Tori?" I hear my mom say.

As she gets up and heads toward me, I shift to give her room to sit beside me. "Tori, honey I was so worried. What happened? Whatever it is we can face it together, I swear."

"I know mom."

There is rustling on the floor and Charlie sits up, seeing the rest of us are awake.

Now is the time to fill them in on what happened at the diner. Taking a deep breath and doing my best to contain my nerves, I begin. "Last night at dinner I heard a laugh, one I will never ever forget. It was the same laugh as…" I don't have to finish because they know. I can see when the realization hits their faces. I also see the anger immediately cross Will's face.

Before Will can say anything my mom beats him to the punch. "You mean to tell me your rapist was at the same place as you were?"

I nod my head, "I didn't see him, I only heard him."

"Oh honey," my mom begins, "We have to find him. I need to call Detective Harrison."

"I know mom."

"I'll be right back," she says as she rushes off to make the call and Charlie trails after her giving Will and I a moment.

"I'm sorry about ruining our date last night." I feel awful and hang my head in dismay. I was so looking forward to it.

"Hey, look at me. You didn't ruin anything, that piece of shit garbage did."

Clinging to hope, I ask the question that's weighing heavily on my mind. "Did you see his face?"

Shaking his head he says, "I didn't, my eyes were on you the whole time, but I noticed someone sitting with Ashley."

That's right. I remember hearing her laugh and then…

I shiver without realizing it.

"Are you cold?" Will scoots over and tucks me into his side with his arm thrown around me.

I snuggle into him and whisper, "Cold? No, just remembering,"

My mom marches into the room with a pissed-as-hell look on her face, still gripping the phone and Charlie following on her heels. "So, here's the bad news. They can't do a damn thing because there's still no evidence." Mocking the detective's explanation, she 'air quotes', "A laugh doesn't constitute evidence." "I know, even though you only heard his laugh and didn't see his face, that you are one hundred percent sure it was him. Otherwise, you wouldn't have reacted the way you did last night." Frustrated, she throws herself into the recliner.

Will pipes up, "There has to be a way. I can't believe he was that close and I didn't see his face."

Pieces of information and various thoughts fly around my brain, but one thought is abundantly clear to me, "I have to talk to Ashley. I know we don't know for sure if that's who she was with, but I still have to warn her. I can't stand her, but I wouldn't wish what happened to me on my worst enemy."

She laughed and then he laughed, it just makes sense.

"I'll go with you" Will says.

Turning to Will, I place my hand on his cheek and he leans into my palm, "No, this is something I have to do on my own. You know as well as I do she'll respond better if it's just me. I don't want it to seem like we're ganging up on her. But, thank you for the offer."

He smiles a sad smile knowing I'm right, but I can tell he doesn't like it. Turning his head, he kisses the palm of my hand. "You are the bravest girl I know."

That is probably the best compliment that he could give me. Before all of this, hearing I looked nice was enough, but now, being brave has a whole new meaning. I smile warmly at him before turning to my mom and Charlie. "Last night I heard him and just shut down. I couldn't think of anything else."

Charlie, who's been quiet this whole time, speaks up. "You were in shock T. I could see it all over you. Not until you knew that you were completely safe did you finally calm down and fall asleep."

"I was a mess." I shake my head, vaguely recalling the previous night. "I just knew I had to get away and get home. When I heard him, it was like a bucket of ice cold water being dropped on me and I couldn't move, like being frozen in place. I had to force my feet to move. This morning, though, waking up and seeing the three of you here with me, I feel safe and protected. I feel I can face anything after last night. Maybe next time I'll handle it better?" Doubt makes my voice turn it into a question. I *want* to believe I can handle it better. When he's caught, I know I want to confront him. I have to do this for me. I need to see it through to the very end.

Will stays for the rest of the day hanging with my family and me. It's nice just lounging around the house, watching movies. I feel normal. Normal is something I haven't felt in a very long time.

All rational thought sometimes gets flushed down the toilet

Chapter 33

Will

I spend the day with Tori and her family. It's comfortable and I feel like a permanent part of her life. I need to go home, but even after spending the day with her, I'm not ready to leave.

I knew something happened at the diner, I just didn't know what. Tori, is my number one priority, and when she panicked, everything else fell away. I moved on instinct: *Get her home; keep her safe*. But now, the whole drive home I can't stop thinking about the fact that I was in the same place as *him*. I want to bash his head in and make him pay for what he did to Tori and possibly others…. My ringing phone cuts through the fury and I answer it without checking the caller id.

"Are you okay, bro?" Not giving me a chance to respond, Maverick continues, "Charlie called and told me. I would've called sooner, but I didn't want to intrude. Charlie said you were spending the day with them. It's good you were there."

"It's not me you should be worried about, it's *him* that's going to need help when I find out who the sack of shit is." I pause before continuing, "Did Charlie tell you Tori's going to try talking to Ashley tomorrow?"

"She mentioned it. I don't know if Ashley will listen but that's all that she can do. Ashley's hard headed and, unfortunately, I can see her doing the opposite out of spite. But all Tori can do is try and she's doing the right thing."

"I'm actually really glad you called. This is killing me Maverick: Tori not knowing I saw her that night. It's eating at me and I can't continue holding onto it."

Maverick sighs into the phone, "This is really bad timing, but I don't think there will ever be good timing, not for something like this."

It makes me angry just thinking about it and a little too forcefully I say, "Trust me, I know! I'm scared shitless about telling her. She's trusted me enough to fall asleep on me. She trusts me to keep her safe. Hell, she trusted me enough to let me hold her while she was in shock and scared out of her mind. I can't keep this to myself; I can't move forward with secrets between us."

Maverick's quiet for a moment before saying, "I know bro, but be prepared. Be prepared for her to be pissed and hurt. It is the right thing to do but…"

"I know, and already know I may lose her entirely and it terrifies the hell out of me."

"Will, I don't think you're going to lose her, but I do think she's going to be pissed as hell and hurt beyond words. If she loves you the way I think she does, she'll come around."

"God, I hope you're right."

"Dude, you really should listen to me more, I'm usually right."

I chuckle a little, "Yeah, whatever. Actually, isn't it usually me instilling the words of wisdom? Somehow the roles have been reversed. I don't know how *that* happened!"

"It's the girls," Maverick says. "They screw with our brain so we can't think straight, and when you find the right one, all rational thought gets flushed down the toilet."

"Isn't that the truth," I mutter.

"When are you going to tell her?" he asks.

"I'll wait a day or two after she speaks to Ashley. She's going to need me afterwards."

"Yeah she is," he sighs. "Holler if you need me. I'll see you at school tomorrow."

We hang up, but I don't feel any better. Even with Maverick's so called words of wisdom. Tomorrow I'll be there for her and then after that...after that we need to talk. I just hope she knows how much I love her.

Little by little, piece by piece

Chapter 34

Tori

I'm getting ready for school with only thoughts of Ashley in my head. I know, not good right? Who wants to wake up thinking about Ashley? Definitely not me.

I greet Charlie downstairs, "Hey Char, I'm driving today. I've got an appointment with the Doc today. Actually, timing couldn't be better after the weekend I've had, and with today…."

"Are you sure you don't want me with you when you speak to 'the bitch'?"

I tilt my head to the side and can't stop the smirk quickly forming at the use of the nickname I gave Ashley. Some things stick, what can I say?

"Naw, I got it. I need to do this. You know she's not a fan of ours. One of us talking to her is bad enough but two? More importantly, both of us having to endure that kind of torture—well that's just not right," I intone sarcastically.

Charlie throws her head back and laughs, "You've got a point but…I would endure it for you. If you need me I'll be there right along with you."

"Thanks babe, but I got it." I reply, with a hip-bump for emphasis.

We head off to school and meet the guys in the parking lot. Will seems off this morning and I can't quite put my finger on it. I mean he's happy to see me and grabs my hand immediately, but there's just something…off.

"When are you going to talk to her?" Will asks.

"I dunno, I was thinking at lunch. I can take her aside and talk to her with a little more privacy. Especially not knowing how she's going to react."

He nods his head and looks around before turning back to me, "I'll be here when you need me."

"I know," I say warmly.

I bump him a little to get his attention. "What's wrong? You seem, I don't know, a little off today."

He quickly tries to hide it, "I'm just a little tired; that's all."

"Maybe you should have gone home sooner yesterday and gotten more sleep?"

He throws his arm around me, pulling me close to whisper in my ear, "There is no place I would have rather been than with you yesterday. I loved spending the entire day with you. Waking up with you in my arms, and spending the entire day snuggling on the couch—No, that was perfect."

A shiver runs down my back at his words and, more specifically, his nearness. The good kind of shiver. I pull away a bit so I can reach up and kiss him on the cheek, then whisper, "Thank you."

His eyes sparkle and dance, but there's a hint of sadness. I decide to let it go; convinced I'm imagining it. He's just tired, like he says.

I go about my day constantly looking at the time, dreading my conversation with Ashley. She's never been a pleasant person to speak with. Not sure what I ever did to deserve her wrath, she's just never liked me and it's okay. I know it's unrealistic to get along with everyone, but there's just always been hostility about her I could never figure out. It's like I'd done something without ever realizing it. I sigh when the bell rings signaling the next class, knowing it's lunchtime.

Oh joy, show time!

I make my way to the lunchroom and decide to just get it over with; do it prior to eating. I catch Will's eye and indicate I'm going over. I feel like I'm in a James Bond movie, for crying out loud. I search the room for Ashley and spot her at her table already. Taking the deepest breath of my life, I walk over to her. Beside her is the 'other bitch'—I mean Miranda. I get to the table and wait to be acknowledged. Finally Ashley looks up, "Lost Tori? 'Cause you sit over there." She literally points to my table. I glance over to see Will, Maverick and Charlie all staring at me.

Okay guys, obvious much?

When they all notice that they've been had, they instantly look away. Busted, they each quickly glance randomly away. I inwardly, chuckle, and feel a little better; a bit more at ease with the impending conversation. "Can we talk Ashley? It'll only take a second."

"What could you possibly need to talk to me about?" She asks snidely.

Count to ten Tori. I take a slow cleansing breath. I want to bite her head off but it wouldn't solve a damn thing, or help her. "We could have this conversation here but I don't think you're going to like it. I suggest we speak in private.

She huffs out a deep breath, obviously put-out, "Fine, but make it quick."

Yeah, because I so badly want to spend my lunch time talking to your sour puss self.

She reluctantly follows me out of the cafeteria and we walk to a quiet corner in the hallway. She turns around with her arms crossed, "What do you have to say?"

"Who were you with Saturday night at the diner?"

She smirks and gets the old 'holier than thou' look on her face. "Why? Ready to trade in Will in already?"

"Not hardly." There's an edge to my voice that I can't help. This girl pushes my buttons in so many different ways. "Just tell me Ashley, who was he?"

"Why? Jealous? I have something you want, Tori?"

"For the last damn time, Ashley, I don't want him! Let me give you a piece of advice. Be careful of your date, whoever he is. He hurts people, girls specifically."

"Why would you say this?" She shouts at me.

"Because it's true, and if you're smart, you'll stay away from him!"

She smiles—of all things, "I can't believe it. You finally want someone that's with me. This is rich! Well, sorry to disappoint, but you can't have him!"

Exasperated, I raise my voice, "Oh. My. God. For the last time, I don't want him. I'm just warning you he's not a good guy, and continuing to see him isn't the smartest thing to do! I'm trying to *help* you, but you refuse to listen! I'm not in competition with you Ashley, and I never have been. I'm telling you, he's bad news and he could hurt you. That's all. Do what you want Ashley, you're going to anyway." Finished with my 'good deed' I march away and leave her standing there. I did what I could and the rest is up to her, whether she believes me or not.

Furious, I'm shaking as I make my way back into the cafeteria and our table and slump down next to Will.

"It went that good, huh?" Will asks.

"Smashing. Can't you tell?"

Charlie leans closer, "Well, you did what you could, ya know."

"Yeah," I sigh. "She kept saying I wanted the guy she was dating, and I'm obviously not happy being with Will." Will chokes on his drink and nearly spits it everywhere, which almost makes me laugh. Almost. "Oh, and she finally had something I wanted. I mean, what the hell? I told her it wasn't a competition. Ugh, she makes me so furious!"

Will throws an arm over my shoulder, "I'm still proud of you, regardless of how she took it."

I lean into him a little more, "Thanks. I knew it wasn't going to be pleasant, and I certainly wasn't looking forward to it, but damn Gina!" I whine, causing everyone else to burst out laughing.

"Go ahead and laugh." I watch them laugh and I can't help the smile that creeps onto my face. "Glad I could provide entertainment."

Unexpectedly, Charlie blurts, "There she is! The Tori we all miss and love is coming back."

Yeah, I am. Little by little; piece by piece I'm coming back.

Not gone, but easier

Chapter 35

Tori

Therapy gets easier the more you go. Especially when she already knows your darkest secret. I don't feel judged and it's easier to discuss the mishaps that come and go along the way. I explained what happened over the weekend and how I handled it; or didn't. At least not well. I did, indeed, have a panic attack, and Dr. Heart wasn't surprised at my reaction. On the positive side she pointed out that by leaning on Will, I demonstrated the immense level of trust I have in him, which is a very good sign. I guess that means I'm not completely broken after all.

I told her about warning Ashley and how poorly the conversation went. She asked why Ashley felt the need to push my buttons and 'felt' the need for competition. I joked that while I didn't have a clue, I'd be more than happy to pass along her card. I'm sure she needs as much as help as me, if not more. Dr. Heart actually quirked a small smile at that. I'm finally able to joke more and more, and I feel more and more like my old self. My nightmares are even getting easier; not gone, but easier.

Will's still acting strange and says he needs to speak to me about something. Surely it can't be anything big because he's still affectionate and always holding my hand, or making out with my head. Okay, not really, but you know what I mean. He's bringing dinner over tonight and we are going to 'talk' afterwards. I'm not sure what's in store, but I'm really hoping for no surprises. I don't think I can handle any.

While I'm waiting for Will to show up, I pull out my guitar and bring it into the living room. I always pick and choose songs based on my mood in the moment. I'm feeling so much better than I have in such a long time, that my song choices are lighter. Charlie sits up when she sees what's in my hand. Like an excited child she claps her hands together, "Oh can I choose a song?" I love her excitement over the small things, one of her best qualities.

"What are you thinking?" I like some pop music, but country music is what I was brought up on. Charlie tends to bounce between genres, so I'm curious what she'll pick.

"What about *Crazy* by Hunter Hayes?"

"Aw, Charlie's in a playful mood is she? Want to harmonize with me? This is gonna be fun, I love that song."

She moves closer to the end of the couch, excitement coming off of her in waves. I love how she loves music as much as I do. I begin playing and get lost in the music. I can't help the smile on my face and she's sporting the same one. It's fast paced and fun and we're sounding pretty damn good—our voices so very different, but sound so damn good together, blending perfectly.

I don't want good and I don't want good enough. Can't sleep, can't breathe without your love. Front porch and one more kiss. It doesn't make sense to anybody else.

The chorus is the most fun part and we hit, and time it perfectly. Why didn't we do this before?

All of a sudden, we hear clapping. We turn around surprised and see mom and Will standing in the doorway with a look of pure astonishment.

"Oh my God, girls, that was freaking fantastic!" She says with a massive grin.

"Really?" I ask.

"Hell yeah, it was spectacular!" Will exclaims.

"Holy shit, that was fun," Charlie beams before ducking her head and glancing at my mom with a hint of remorse at her use of the word 'shit'.

"That was the most fun I've had, like ever," I laugh.

Overflowing with pride, my mom says, "The blending of Charlie's angelic voice and your raspy voice—it just sounds awesome! Y'all should think about getting a gig, or two. It was that good!"

I can't quit smiling. and one glance a Charlie reveals she's the same way. We look at each other and start giggling like twelve year olds. "Hmm Char, we may need to see about taking our act on the road. What do you think about that?"

Charlie nods her head empathically, "I think yes!"

"Cool!"

I notice Will, and I am struck by how hot he is leaning against the doorway—looking way to cool for his own good. I feel so good, and brave; possibly too brave for my own good.

"Are you hungry?"

Will's question sends my brain spinning in a whole new direction and I think, *"Yeah, but not for food."*

Thank the Lord I don't say that out loud. What the hell is wrong with me?

He brought enough food for the four of us. We take it into the living room and the subject of Charlie and I singing together works its way back into the conversation. We talk about where we could get gigs, and what our duo name would be, which turns the conversation in to a game to come up with a name, and everything gets thrown on the table from stupid to very stupid. But, who cares? It was fun.

Chapter 36

Will

I pull Tori to her feet and ask if we can talk. God, I hate doing this, especially when we were having a great time. She finally seems happy and here I am about to ruin the whole evening. I know she can sense my sudden unease and she's hesitant, but she still takes my hand, following me outside to the porch swing. I shut the door behind us and follow her to the swing, sitting beside her.

"Will, you're kinda freaking me out a bit. What's going on?"

God, where do I start?

"There's something I have to tell you. Something I've been scared to tell you, but I don't want any secrets between us. I want us to have an open and honest relationship and I can't do that unless I'm completely honest with you."

"Way to start off the conversation, Will, you succeeded in scaring me."

"I know, fuck. I don't know how to say it and I'm screwing it up."

"Please, just say it," Tori pleads.

I hate seeing her upset knowing I've caused it. One minute she's laughing her ass off and the next I've upset her. I hold her gaze she can see the absolute truth in my words. "Please know that I love you. I've never loved anyone else, only you. It's always been you." I sigh and begin, "That night at the party we went to, I saw you."

"What do you mean you saw me? How could you have seen me? I was in that damn truck."

Shame fills me, "When I'd been looking for you, I saw you sitting in the truck and the door was wide open. I saw you and promptly turned around and left."

Her voice quivers, "What do you mean you left? If you saw me why would you leave?"

I don't say anything for a few seconds and I see recognition sink in and she gets it. "You thought I willingly had sex with him?" Her eyes get misty and the seal breaks as tears finally begin to fall. "You honestly thought I was the kind of girl that would show up at a party with a guy she's liked for *so long* and leave with another to have sex?"

Filled with shame, I look away. "I don't know what I was thinking. I just saw you in the truck and I left. I was upset and thought maybe I liked you more than you liked me and…" I can't finish, because the more I talk, the more I sound like an asshole. "I'm so sorry Tori, I…"

Cutting me off, "If you'd waited around long enough, you would have seen him push my ass out the door to land on the ground like a piece of garbage because he was done with me. He even *dismissed* me, saying I could now go. If you had waited just a few more seconds and you would have *seen* it."

God, what have I done? I begin to scoot closer to her, but she moves out of my reach and stands up. "Tori, I love you so much and I'm sorry I was such a fucking idiot. I didn't think. I couldn't keep this from you any longer and I should have told you sooner."

With anger I've never seen aimed at me, and tears I haven't seen since the night at the lake she seethes, "You're damn right you should have. I can't believe the guy I thought I knew and loved thought so little of me. Will you need to leave; I need you to go, now!"

I've never openly cried, but I can't stop the tears that slip down my face, and I don't bother to hide them. "I'm sorry, Tori; I know I fucked up. If I could change it I would, I swear to God I would." I turn and leave, respecting her request. The further I walk away from her, the more I feel I've lost her and I can't blame it on anyone but myself, not this time. No, this time it's all on me.

Aftermath

Chapter 37

Tori

With tears streaking down my face, I watch Will leave. He looks back once with pain and remorse carved on his face, then turns back towards his truck and leaves. I'm not sure how long I stay outside before Charlie comes to check on me.

"Tori, are you still out here?" She spots me crying and sits down beside me, comforting me. "What's wrong, and where's Will? Why did he leave?"

Struggling to pull myself together because I can't fall apart again, I tell myself to be strong and I tell her what he told me. It's clear she didn't know and she is genuinely shocked just as I am. We walk into the house and I drop on the couch, literally spent and exhausted. I feel I've run out of tears and honestly, I don't want to cry anymore.

Charlie sits in the chair across from me and shakes her head as she says, "Wow, I didn't see that coming. I just can't believe it."

I feel so lost at this point. Will is such a huge part of my life and support system. I love him. "How could he have thought I would do that? I've never given him any indication that I was even like that. Why?" My mind is completely boggled and I can't seem to make any sense of it.

"How did he seem afterwards?" Charlie asks.

"Like an ass, of course. He felt really bad, as he should." I feel tears begin to threaten all over again. Apparently, I'm not out of tears after all.

"I know you're trying to be strong and think you're weak if you let them fall, but you're not weak. You're allowed to be upset, Tori." She knows me so well. I don't doubt she speaks from personal experience. She comes to sit, cross-legged, next to me. "What are you going to do?"

"I haven't even thought about it that far, yet." I look at her, "I can't be with someone who thinks so low of me. How am I supposed to get past this?" I am absolutely defeated.

"I think you shouldn't make any rash decisions just yet."

"This was more than I bargained for right now, and I have to focus on me." A couple tears make their way down my cheek and I harshly wipe them away. Despite Charlie's reassurances, I feel weak for letting them escape.

"You're strong T, stronger than you give yourself credit for. I know we keep telling you, but you are. And I'll keep telling you until you finally believe it."

"How did this day go from awesome to shitastic in a nano second?" I ask shaking my head. "I mean one moment we're laughing and singing having a great time and in the next…"

"I'm sorry, I really am. Can I say something without you biting my head off?" She asks tentatively.

"Um yeah," I say wearily.

"Remember Maverick after his accident, and how stupid he was to push me away?"

"How could I forget Char? He was a douche-bag and I had to knock some sense into him."

"If there's one thing I learned from that experience it's that guys are just stupid sometimes and do the most idiotic things."

I open my mouth to interrupt her, but she throws her hand up shushing me. "I'm not discounting what he did, and yeah, you should be pissed; I'm pissed. Just remember he's probably beating himself up about his stupidity, too."

I take a moment to consider her words, but it hurts to think about it anymore tonight. My brain needs a break.

"I'll think about it, but not tonight, I need to go to bed."

She throws her arm around me gives me a hug. "Night, T."

"Night babe, love ya," I say as I start up the stairs to my room.

I hear her holler, "Love ya back."

Once I'm in my room, I waste no time changing into my pajamas and get ready for bed. I see my cell phone sitting on the table by the bed with a light flashing, signaling I have a message. I grab it and notice the message is from Will. Apparently, I must enjoy torture because I decide to listen to it.

Tori, I'm… I'm so sorry. Please believe me. I love you so much and I hope you can forgive me. I didn't want to have any secrets between us, and even though I knew it would hurt you, I took the chance because…SHIT. I'm saying this all wrong…I just want you to know I'll always be here for you. I'll always love you. I've loved you for so long, longer than you think, way before we were ever together. I need you to know I didn't intend to hurt you, but you needed to know. I know you're not that kind of girl; I don't know why it was my first thought. Please know I'm just…sorry. I hope you can find a way to forgive me, I really do. I love you, Tori.

By the end of the message, I'm a weepy mess. I lay down and listen to it again.

Now I know I like personal punishment.

I finally lay my phone down and yank the covers up, giving myself over to sleep with tear filled eyes. It takes several minutes, my mind wandering, but I finally let go. The last image that runs through my head is Will; it's always Will.

Guys are stupid and idiotic

Chapter 38

Will

I knew it would be bad.

Shit!

I call Maverick and tell him how it went, which obviously isn't well. He tries, he really does but there isn't anything to be said to make me feel better. I decide the only thing that's going to make me feel better is knowing we've gotten rid of that bastard. I tell Maverick I'm picking him up without giving him a choice.

On my way to Maverick's, I leave Tori a message, but I know I need to give her time. I have to remind myself constantly.

Time. She just needs time.

Maverick is waiting for me outside when I pull into his driveway. Getting in he scoffs, "Damn Will, I know you're upset, but I need my beauty sleep."

I throw him a semi-smirk but then he says, "Charlie called me."

This can only mean one thing: Tori spoke to Charlie. I knew she would but… Hell, I don't know what I thought. "And? Does she hate me, too?"

"You know she doesn't have it in her to hate you. She can't even hate her own parents. No, she's pissed you thought that about Tori, but she did talk to Tori."

I'm not sure if this is a good, or a bad, thing.

Attempting to clear my throat of my nervousness I ask, "Oh, and what did she tell her?"

"She called you stupid and idiotic, but the conversation was in your favor."

"How can calling me stupid and idiotic be in my favor?" This I've got to hear.

"She said sometimes guys do stupid and idiotic things, and we don't know why. But, Charlie also said she was sure you didn't really think Tori would just hop in a truck with someone else, after starting the evening with you. Hence, we do stupid and idiotic things. She also brought up how I acted after my accident and pushed her away. As if I want to *ever* be reminded about that. She does have a point, you know. I'm not even offended because she's right," he says with a snort. "Where are we going by the way?"

"I thought we might ride by Ashley's house and see if she has 'company'."

Maverick agrees, "Dude, not a bad idea. It can't hurt."

"You never know. I figure if we see a truck in the driveway, we can narrow it down. Her dad may have a truck, but I know the truck we're looking for is an older model."

Shocked to hear this tidbit of information he asks, "How do you know that?"

I sigh loudly.

"Will, I already know what happened, you need to just tell me. You know I will never say anything. I'm helping you look for the douche-bag, so I need to know."

I'm not worried about him saying anything; rather, it's about Tori's privacy, and what she may, or may not, want him to know. I decide to be as vague as possible. "Tori's hands were held above her head." Anger surges through me as I finish, "They dug into the window handle."

Maverick turns, anger reverberating off him, "Just so you know, we are taking turns with that sick son-of-a-bitch."

"Yeah, I figured you'd want to. Okay, I'm just going to drive by slowly," I say. "Keep an eye out so no one thinks we're a couple of perverts on a stroll."

We drive by and there's only a single light on in a room. The house is quiet, and nope, no truck to be seen.

"Well that blows," Maverick says.

"We aren't stopping until he's caught. I have to do this, if only for Tori's peace of mind."

We get out of dodge and Maverick says, "You know she can't be mad at you forever. You've been through so much together and I know she loves you. Hell anybody around you can tell. It's sickening."

"Holy shit *Mav*." I say, using Charlie's pet name in a girly tone. "You're one to talk. Are you kidding? Watching you two made me want to throw up. How do you think Tori and I felt all these months? God, it was awful." I shiver for added effect.

Maverick throws his head back laughing, "Yeah, yeah. I get what you're saying. But bro, really, you can tell she cares and that doesn't go away easily, and definitely not overnight."

"I hope you're right."

I drop Maverick at home, thanking him. I went from being upset, hurt and pissed at myself to feeling slightly better, thanks to Maverick. If she can't forgive me right now then that's fine, but I sure as hell am not giving up easily. Hell no.

The bitch brings out the bitch in me

Chapter 39

Tori

The last couple of days before my weekend begins I avoid Will like the plague at school, as best I can anyway. Obviously, I can't completely stay away, but despite my efforts to avoid all eye contact, my eyes betray me. I see yearning etched on his face, and I'm sure my expression mirrors his. When we arrive at school I want so desperately to go up to him and say I forgive you and I love you. But it's still too raw and I'm just not there, yet. I already miss the hand holding. That seemingly inconsequential touch gives me just enough courage to make it through the day. I've come to rely on him and it, maybe too much. I would give anything to forget last night's conversation, just pretend it never happened, but I can't.

The bitches, especially Ashley, notice the tension between Will and me. I catch her smirking, and I try to pretend it doesn't bother me. But I have a hard time not showing my feelings and placing them on display on my shoulder. You'd be blind not to see it. I notice her giving Will the 'eyes' several times throughout the day. I even had to stop myself once from going over and clawing her eyes out. The topper on the cake was when she walked over to him, but caught my attention first and gave me an "it's my turn, now" look. I swear, to all that is holy, it took everything in me to hold myself back. That time I needed Charlie. Actually, I think Charlie would've been happy to join me in the ass-kicking, if it hadn't been for Maverick shaking his head no. The whole scene would have been comical on any other day. Not today though, clearly. Although, I could tell Maverick was doing everything possible to reign in the smile trying to force itself out. What can I say? The *bitch* brings out the 'bitch' in me.

Charlie decides to stay in with me tonight and tomorrow. She says something about the guys having plans with the team, but Maverick and she have plans all day Sunday. I think she feels sorry for me, but I'm trying not to spend too much time over-analyzing it; I'm just enjoying the time with my best friend, trying to forget. The plan is to hang out at home vegging out and watching movies all day.

Finally, the school day comes to a close, and I can't get out of there fast enough. Charlie and I are walking out together when Ashley decides to join us.

Really? Is she asking for punishment?

While I try my best to pretend she's invisible, I see Charlie glance over at her with a confused look on her face, "Um, Ashley are you needing something?"

With the snarkiest of looks she chirps, "No, I just wanted to ask what you did to lose Will already."

"Are you kidding me, Ashley?" I stop dead. "Why do you have to be such a bitch?"

"Well y'all didn't last long, and I'm thinking of going for him myself. My other guy may not work out."

"Yeah, cause he's a winner." I can't help but mutter.

"Whatever," Ashley says. "I may just have both."

I know damn well Will can't stand her. "Give it your best shot, Ashley. Really, I wish you luck," I snark back.

She takes this as a challenge because her eyes get big and begin to sparkle. "Watch me, Tori. Just you wait; I'll have him all over me before you know it."

OMG, I've created a monster! I so want to slap her.

I know Will isn't in to her, but still it causes my stomach to do flip-flops. I'm always going to have that 'what if' feeling in the pit of my stomach.

"Go, Ashley. Get the hell away and find someone else to bug," Charlie bites at her.

I see her mosey her way over to Will. He glances up at her and they strike up a conversation.

Charlie nudges me in the shoulder. "Ignore her, T, remember this is Will we're talking about."

I nudge her back and sigh, "Yeah, I know."

We stop at the grocery store on the way home, loading up on enough junk food to last the entire weekend and stop for movies.

That is how we spend our Friday night. All junked out on food, watching movies that make us laugh and cry the entire night.

Madder than a hornets nest

Chapter 40

Will

The last couple of days have been hell. Seeing Tori at school and not talking to her sucks some major ass. I wanted to, trust me. Several times I was tempted to walk over to her, but stayed away. I know she needs time. I just wish she knew how terribly sorry I am. I want so desperately to hold her. I didn't miss the look of disdain on Tori's face when Ashley decided to torment her by talking to me. At least I know she isn't completely over me, and her irritation gives me some hope, as sick as that sounds. Hope that maybe, just maybe, she can get past this.

Maverick and I spend Friday night with the guys, something we always do as it gets closer to the end of school. The team gets together and we hang for the whole weekend being stupid. Normally, girlfriends are invited but Charlie, being the good friend she is, didn't want to leave Tori alone. Charlie doesn't know how much I appreciate it; I hate the thought of Tori being home alone.

If Charlie had been with us Friday night she would've been pissed as hell. Ashley's advances were insane. Charlie would have, without a doubt, clawed that girl's eyes out. In fact, I had to take Ashley aside and tell her where I stood. It was a pretty simple conversation: "I love Tori, and I'm not over her, not by a long shot. You need to back the hell off." She just fluttered and batted her eyes and moved on to the next guy. Ty was all over her. I even got a thumbs up from him as he was smiling like a fool. I walked away smiling and knowing that at least I was safe for the rest of the evening from her craziness. I left when Maverick did. It just wasn't fun without Charlie and Tori. Yeah, I know I'm holding on to some major faith.

Here we go again, I think to myself, another evening with the guys. Should be fun, right? It's what every guy wants: his space and to just hang with his 'bro's'. Nope, I'd rather spend it curled on the couch with Tori, watching a movie.

Saturday we head to the public area of the lake to meet up with everyone. Thankfully, it's away from our regular spot; don't want it tarnished by all the crap going on tonight.

The public area is a small part of the beach with a circular pit for a bonfire. Some of the guys arrive early to start it up, but Maverick and me—hell no. We're only going to hang out with the guys because it's our last hoorah and that's it. I don't even plan on being here late tonight, to be honest.

Maverick and I shoot the shit, hob-knobbing with the guys for a couple of hours. Some are sloshed out of their minds. I see guys and girls I've never seen before. So much for being a team thing. I'm so ready to get out of here. I glance at Maverick and see the same look reflected on his face. Thank the Lord above, he's ready to go, too. We make our goodbyes, catch a little crap and get called a few names that would probably make Charlie blush. Not Tori, though. No, my Tori would have a response for his crass mouth and that causes me to smile and chuckle.

"What are you laughing at?"

"Just thinking about what Josh just called us. You know damn well if the girls were with us, Charlie would blush and Tori would have a comeback ready for his sorry mouth."

Maverick laughs, throwing his head back, "You're right, and I can picture it, too."

"I miss her so much, and it's only been a couple of days." We walk to Maverick's car among the scattered vehicles.

"I understand that," Maverick agrees. "When I was a part from Charlie I felt the same way. I get it. I…"

"Shhh," I cut him off. "Did you hear that?"

Maverick and I stop walking and listen. We hear faint noises that sound like muffled screams. "I think it's this way," I say.

Maverick follows and we come to a faded burgundy truck. The windows are fogged up and it's rocking a little.

"Maybe we should give them their privacy," Maverick says and turns to walk away.

Reaching out my hand, I stop him. "No! Something's wrong. I feel it in my gut." My heart begins to beat fast and instinct tells me not to leave. All of a sudden, I see a hand slap the window and nails drag its way down, followed by another, much bigger hand yanking it away. Then everything snaps into focus. The older truck…I see it in my mind from a year ago…I remember! My vision floods red and all I see is Tori. I rush over to the truck and yank the door open. Despite all logic, I expect to see Tori in the truck. An unfamiliar guy is laid over her and her shirt is pulled up. His hands are roaming in places they shouldn't be. The tear-streaked face I see is Tori. I hear a whimper as I pull the girl out as gently as I can. Maverick grabs the girl and as they move away, I faintly register him asking if she's okay.

The guy looks at me with a sick, twisted smile on his face. "We were just having a little fun. She wants me, and she likes it rough." For the first time in my life, I'm looking at someone and cannot see one trace of good in him. This guy is pure evil, and he needs to be stopped!

Dumbstruck, and still seeing red, I suddenly have the urge to pound him to within an inch of his life. Faster than I can register what I'm doing, I rush to his side of the truck, throw open the door and yank his ass out. He's laughing like it's a joke, not taking me seriously, and he just succeeds in getting me madder than a hornet's nest. He smirks at me—fucking smirks! Pulling my arm back, I throw it forward with every ounce of strength I possess. He staggers from the punch, while pain radiates down my arm but I don't give a shit, and I punch him again. He finally falls to the ground and crouching over him, I continue beating him until, finally, I'm yanked away. I sit on the ground, staring. The sack of shit just lies on the ground, not moving as a paramedic leans over him. After a few minutes, I feel a hand resting on my shoulder, and I faintly hear someone trying to get my attention. Finally, I get a thump to the back of the head, snapping me back to the present.

"What the hell?" I whip my head around to see Maverick standing over me.

"Dude, you were supposed to leave me a punch, but no, you had to take care of it all on your own."

"How is she?"

"Oh you mean Ashley?"

"Ashley?" I ask surprised.

"That's who was in the car. It was Ashley."

"How is she?" I ask, my voice unsteady.

"She's been smacked around. She has a black eye and I don't know..." He trails off.

I know where he's going, and it's not something I want to think about.

I release the breath I'm holding and finally feel the pain in my hand. It hurts like a son of a bitch.

"Come on slugger, let's get you looked at."

I walk over to the paramedic and a police officer makes his way over introducing himself. "After your hand is looked at, I'm going to need you to come into the station."

I nod my head, but the paramedic interjects, "Not before he goes to the hospital to get his hand treated." Turns out, I broke my hand. It was worth it.

Maverick tells the paramedic he'll drive me, and we head back to his car. The moment we get in he asks, "What do we do from here?"

"What do you mean? The guy has been caught, which is what we wanted, right?"

He quickly glances over, "No, about letting Tori know what's going on; that her rapist has been caught."

"Actually bro, first we have to make sure it's the same guy. *I* think it is, and *you* think it is, but... and I really hope I'm right because I just beat the tar out of him which he deserved anyway....Seeing the truck brought back the memory of seeing Tori in it, and it was familiar. I know it has to be him, but I'm not calling anyone until we know for sure. Honestly, I think she needs to hear it from the police."

"You're right," Maverick says. "I still can't believe you didn't save me a punch. What kind of friend are you?" he says laughing. "You gave it to him good to. Even though you hurt yourself in the process."

My mind falls back to Tori and all I can think about is this guy is caught and she doesn't have to fear her attacker is going to hurt her or anyone else again. I'm so relieved at the thought.

We get to the waiting room and Maverick asks, "Let me see your hand."

I unwrap the gauze and ice, wincing, and take a look. It's a purple plump mass and looks completely disfigured.

"Nasty. Maybe it's a good thing I didn't punch him. I've already got a bum knee," Maverick jokes.

"Asshole." I mutter.

After sitting for what seems like hours, I'm finally called in, and they let Maverick join me because he's a witness. Not long after, a detective in plain clothes comes in with a uniformed officer. "Hi, I'm Detective Harrison, and you are?"

We give him our names and recall the events of the night. I go first since I did the punching.

"I didn't know what was going on. We heard a muffled scream and a hand hit the window. The nails started sliding down the glass as if in duress. I acted on instinct and opened the door. I could tell she was upset and yanked his ass out and punched him. He laughed at first and though it was funny. Well, it wasn't funny."

Detective Harrison tries to hide his smirk, but I catch it before he's able to regain his composure. I'm generally pretty observant—situations involving Tori notwithstanding—and I pick up on some clues from the detective that put me at ease. One, his sudden smirk tells me it really doesn't bother him that I punched the crap out of the guy, and two, Harrison has to know the guy is guilty, otherwise he would be pissed I knocked him out.

Sensing Harrison is on my side, I take the chance a share, "My girlfriend was attacked a little over a year ago. When I saw the fogged windows, and heard the muffled cry, I just knew it was him. I couldn't allow him to hurt anyone like he hurt Tori." Needing to know if I stopped the attack in time, I ask. "Did he…" I can't finish the sentence, but the detective knows what I'm asking.

"Normally, I wouldn't tell you this, and I'm really not supposed to, but, for your peace of mind….No, he didn't; you stopped him in time."

Waves of relief crash through me with the knowledge he didn't get the chance to do this to someone else.

Maverick goes through his recollection of the evening step by step, and Detective Harrison thanks us for our time and says he'll be in touch. Meanwhile, my hand hurts like hell and I'm informed it needs a cast.

"Great."

Maverick, always looking on the bright side, says jokingly, "Just think, you'll be the talk of the entire school."

"Just what I always wanted," I say sarcastically.

He and I spend another two hours at the hospital before I'm allowed to leave. We still have to stop for a couple of prescriptions, but I'm finally free to go.

I wonder how Ashley's doing, but we don't run it to her on the way out. And, despite her mean-streak, I'm glad she had a better ending than Tori. Although I'm sure the incident will affect her for a while, she's lucky because it could have been much, much worse.

The handsomeness turns ugly

Chapter 41

Tori

I come awake to the sound of the phone ringing and glance at the clock. Holy hell it's early. Seven o'clock on a Sunday morning—really? That's just insane! I turn over in the bed trying to get comfortable again to go back to sleep, but no such luck. I hear feet stomping up the stairs and someone nearing my room. I groan, wanting to go back to sleep. It was a late night of watching movies with ridiculously hot men, and eating tons of junk food. Even my mom got in on the action. I turn my head when I hear someone enter my room and see her walk in. She has a strange look on her face and she's nervous, as if something's wrong.

"What is it? What's wrong? You're scaring me."

She sits down on the bed causing me to sit up. She's ringing her hands fidgeting so much I can tell something is weighing heavily on her mind. "That was

Detective Harrison," she starts. "They think they caught your rapist."

I'm struck dumb. I don't know how I'm supposed to react, let alone think. Conflicting emotions swirl around in my head: I'm elated he's in custody, but I'm scared of what that means for me.

"Okay, what does this mean?"

"It means they need you to go in for a line-up."

Fear immediately engulfs my entire body and I begin to shake. My mom pulls me to her and wraps her arms around me tightly, trying to sooth me and make it better, but this isn't a scrape on the knee, or a broken heart that she can kiss and make better. Lord knows I wish it were. No, this is more. This is the fear of him seeing me, fear of the unknown. But, the fear will never go away if I don't do something to end it. Cautiously, I pull away from her embrace and work to get a hold of myself.

"I'll take a quick shower and get dressed, then we'll go," trying to contain the quiver in my voice, I get up. Forcing bravery I don't feel, I gather my things and walk across the hall to the bathroom—my mom watching silently as I go. I walk in and undress letting the water warm before stepping inside. When I do step in, the warm spray jolts me awake and everything crashes down on me at once. Tears pour down, and I can't stop them. My legs turn to jelly, unable to hold my body up any longer, and I crumble as the warm water cascades over me. As several thoughts run through my mind, I lean my head back and just let the water fall, washing all my tears down the drain. Symbolically, the tears wash away all the ugly, damaged feelings I allowed *him* to hold over me. Negative words tumble through my head and I send them down the drain with my tears. Nothingness. Victim. Powerless. Scared. Used. And many, many more. I let it all go and watch them flow down the drain. I thought I was doing so much better, and in a way I was, but I hadn't let go. I need to let it all go, and refuse to give someone the power to make me feel like I'm nothing ever again. I am so much more. I say it in my head, again and again, until I finally begin to believe it, then I say it once more, out loud:

"My name is Tori. I am no one's victim. And by God, I am a survivor! I've been to hell and back and I. will. heal. I may never forget; but I will never again think about you like I have. I will never give you the power I've been giving you for the last year, and I will never let you hurt anyone else again."

I cry the last tear I will ever shed because of him. Knowing this gives me back the power I've been missing for so very long. Energy begins to course through my body, and I stand up and bathe, finally more whole than I have been in quite some time. When I get out, with the towel wrapped around me, I just stand in front of the mirror. I don't know how to explain it, but I look different, better even. Realization dawns: I finally *believe* the words. I finally believe I'm not nothing, or used, or a victim; I'm me and I'm still whole. I have more color and my eyes—my eyes are different. The overwhelming sadness is gone, so is the hollowness. They reflect the surge of life that is seeping back into me, allowing me to heal and get past this. Something horrific happened to me, something I will never completely get over, and it took me a long time to see it, but I won't let *him* rule or define me. I smile at myself and then open the door, going to my room to get ready with my head held high.

When I'm ready, I walk downstairs to the kitchen where Charlie and my mom are waiting. Charlie's dressed and looks like she's going somewhere. That's right, her date with Maverick, I forgot.

"What are you and Maverick going to do today?"

She looks at me as if I'm crazy. "I'm not. I'm going with you."

"What? No, you haven't spent any of this weekend with him. It's okay, and mom's with me."

Shaking her head, she informs, "Sorry T, but you're stuck with me. I sent a text to Maverick letting him know already. You're not doing this by yourself; no damn way!"

My smile is huge, and I'm so happy I have this fantastic support system, and blessed; yes, I feel blessed.

On the way to the police station I expect to feel nauseous, ready to have my mom pull over so I can up-chuck, but I don't. I'm a little restless and nervous, but holding myself together surprisingly well. Mom assures me Detective Harrison said there's no way he can see me through the mirror. Even though I know this, hearing her say it is a relief.

When we reach the station and we're parked, I find my feet actually moving without having to force them. They carry me in the right direction, following closely behind my mom. I'm still nervous as shit, but I'm ready to do this, nonetheless. My mom speaks to the officer in the front, who directs us to a room. On our way, we pass by another room and I notice the girl inside looks just like Ashley. It can't be Ashley, why would she be here? This girl doesn't look put together like the Ashley I go to school with. No, this one has a black eye and unruly hair and she looks…sad. We reach the line up room and Detective Harrison comes in right after us.

"Hey, Tori. Are you ready to do this?"

No, but yes. I nod to him. Before I can stop myself I blurt, "How did you catch him?"

Detective Harrison looks at me and tilts his head in confusion. "You don't know?"

"No, I really don't know."

He then asks, "Do you know a Will Montgomery?"

My stomach falls and fear overwhelms me. Fear for Will, not for me. I'm scared to know more, but I need to know. "Yes."

"Well, Will and his friend Maverick happened to be at the right place at the right time. They heard some muffled screams and Will took it upon himself to save the girl—just in time, too. He not only saved the girl but Will punched the guy until he lost consciousness, breaking his hand in the process."

I look at Charlie and ask, "Did you know about this?"

The shocked look on her face says it all as she shakes her head no. She had no clue.

Detective Harrison continues, "His friend Maverick called the police while Will was yanking the girl out and beating the guy." He smirks and lightly chuckles, "Your boyfriend was holding onto some major rage to break his hand first punch."

I'm startled by the term boyfriend, and the Detective notices. "He is your boyfriend right? He introduced himself as your boyfriend."

I'm happy to know that he still thinks of me as his girlfriend. Nodding, I say, "He is. He's not in trouble is he? For punching him?"

"No, he saved a girl last night and it could've ended a lot worse."

"What's going to happen now?" I ask.

He sighs in frustration, "We don't have physical evidence from your rape, but it will help if you identify him. Then, with the girl's testimony from last night, and since he was caught in the act with witnesses, we should be able to get him. It's not a perfect system, but my hope is we can find other girls to come forward which will definitely help our case. I don't think you were his first victim, Tori. Are you ready to do this?"

"I am, but I'm not a victim, I'm a survivor." I say proudly, believing it with everything I am.

"I apologize and stand corrected," the detective dips his head in acknowledgement.

The room we walk into is exactly how I've seen it on television, eerily so. The television shows, actually, got this part right. My mom and Charlie stand next to me, as well as Detective Harrison and a uniformed officer. The lights get brighter in the other room and dim slightly in ours. It takes me two seconds to make the identification. Even though I know he can't see my face, I still feel the terror trying to creep in. I look from the first numbered guy to the fifth one as they each step forward. When number four comes forward, I step back a bit. He's beat up, but the grin–the grin gives him away completely. His mouth is slightly upturned in a grin full of secrets that could even be alluring on his handsome face, were it not so sinister. But the handsomeness turns ugly because of the darkness that surrounds him. There's no remorse when I look at him, only enjoyment, like this is a game. As I study him through the mirror, I'm convinced, beyond a shadow of a doubt, he will do it again in a heartbeat. He's a serial rapist. He gets pleasure from hurting women, and he'll continue to do it unless he's stopped.

I hold myself steady and immediately tell them number four. I'm asked if I'm sure several times. They bring each of the other's forward one more time. I repeat, "It's number four. There is absolutely no doubt in my mind it's him. I will never, for as long as I live, forget that face."

We are escorted out and taken back to the first room. "I have to know. Was Ashley, the girl in the other room, his victim?"

"I can't confirm that," he says. "But, I can tell you this: The suspect you positively identified as your rapist is the young lady's attacker from last night. I can also tell you his name is Jason Hoover."

"Jason Hoover," I whisper to no one in particular. Having a name to go with my rapist's face after so long is strange.

We leave the station and as we head home thoughts of Will are running rampant through my mind. How did he catch him? Where was he? Did he know it was Ashley? I realize Will didn't have to act on the noises he heard. He could have ignored them and kept walking last night, minding his own business. But I shake my head to rid the thought from my mind because I know that is not Will. He is brave, and he saved Ashley last night... and with earth shattering clarity everything falls into place. If Will had known what was happening to me when he saw me in the truck, he would have acted differently. Everything I know about him confirms it. But, if Will thought I was there by choice, maybe he walked away because it hurt him to see me there. It still crushes me that he thought I would leave the party with someone else, but I begin to see that his reaction was a testament of his feelings for me.

I ponder this the whole ride home and vow to do something about it.

The road to recovery

Chapter 42

Tori

I fall asleep when I get home. Just as I wake up, the doorbell rings, and I get up to answer it. No one else seems to be around, and the house is quiet. I open the door and, standing before me with a cast on one hand, and kicking something invisible on the ground, is Will. He's so handsome he literally takes my breath away. A lock of hair has fallen in his eyes, but he doesn't shove it away. He peeks out at me from underneath it, his eyes searching mine.

"I know you probably don't want to see me, but the detective called to tell me you'd been by the station. I wanted to make sure you're okay."

All I can think about is having his arms around me, holding me tight. Shaking myself from the thought I respond, "I did, and surprisingly, I'm fine. He told me what you did. I'm sorry you broke your hand. Does it hurt?"

He looks at me with a slight smile, "I have pain pills."

Unable stop my mouth, I say, "You're obviously not taking them because if you were, you wouldn't be here."

"There's my mouthy redhead!" he blurts out. "I've missed her."

Those words remind me just how much I love this guy, and why I need him in my life. He gets me, and appreciates my smart mouth, and Lord knows that doesn't happen often. The thought makes me chuckle and I realize in this moment that it's coming back. I'm coming back.

He notices the change and asks, "You've got a slight smile on your face. Why?"

"I was just thinking you're the only one that actually appreciates my smart mouth. Truth be told, I've realized several things. I know, now, if you had known what was happening to me when you saw me in the truck that night you would have acted differently." I look down at the ground before continuing, "I know your reaction to seeing me, then leaving, was because you had strong feelings for me." I wait just a beat before asking, "Am I wrong?"

Will steps toward me, stopping with just a breath's distance of space between us. "No, Tori, you are definitely not wrong. I wish I never left that night. I've beaten myself up over and over. I was in love with you then but was too chicken to tell you. You are the bravest girl I know."

This is my moment and it's right. I don't feel dread or scared; I feel safe. "Will?" I whisper. "Will you kiss me? But if you kiss me on the forehead again I'm going to slap you."

Will throws his head back and laughs and I can't help continuing, "My forehead has seen way too much action, but these…" I take my fingertip and outline my lips, "these are in need of some long overdue attention."

Will's eyes smolder as he watches my finger. He gently pulls my finger away and threads his hand through mine. I sigh, reveling in the contact I've been missing the last several days. He closes this distance between us, wrapping his other hand around my waist, pulling me tight. "Is this okay?"

"Yes," I barely whisper.

His piercing green eyes never close as he leans over and softly starts to kiss me. I wrap my free arm around his neck, gently caressing the back of his head. He slowly applies more pressure, and I'm in heaven. I swear, if he wasn't holding me, my knees would buckle. I open my mouth and decide to take control, for once. I need this for me. I gently lick his lips and I hear him quietly moan. I slip my tongue inside and gently caress his entire mouth. My body's on fire, with overwhelmingly intense feelings. Physical feelings I haven't felt in so long. Our kisses grow frantic with need and that's when I know. I know that with Will, I'm always safe.

I hear a throat clear and gently pull back still gazing at Will.

"You two need to get a room!"

I can't help it. Maverick sometimes makes me want to beat the shit out of him, but he's so funny that I can't help but burst out laughing. Charlie's with him and slaps him on the arm.

God love her.

"You're such a dick!" Will yells, but he has a smile on his face the entire time. We stand close together with our hands still entwined, smiling and happy.

That night the four of us go swimming at our spot on the lake. I gaze at my boyfriend, staring at all of his hotness, and trust me I notice him staring as well, and we kiss, a lot. I don't freak out and I certainly don't slap him. This time I feel like a normal girl out with her normal, but very hot, boyfriend and finally…finally I'm on the road to recovery.

Epilogue

One month later

Who would have thought in one month's time three girls would come forward and identify Jason Hoover as their rapist? I surely didn't. Detective Harrison says it's a slam dunk and Jason should be put away for quite some time. It is music to my ears. I hope the justice system doesn't fail us; that he'll never be allowed to hurt anyone ever again. Time will tell. One horrible side effect is the media picked up on the story after the girls came forward. It was *the* story for a while and the television stations ate it up. Nothing happens here all that often, and this was big news for our small Podunk town. I never had any evidence to provide the police, unfortunately, due to my year-long wait telling anyone about my rape, but someone else did. Someone who was assaulted that night; someone Will was able to save before the unspeakable deed was done. Ashley's been unable to hide from the media and word got out she was in the truck that night. We aren't sure how, but we never saw her in school, not even on graduation.

Graduation came and went; moving us on to better and bigger things. The four of us spent graduation night together, and mom let us throw a small shindig at our house.

Charlie and I still sing and perform together, and we have a standing gig at the coffee shop. We named our dynamic duo Blessed Hope; a name that holds several special meanings for us. Gaining in popularity, more people are coming out to hear us, and we've been invited to play at other venues in our small town. We're having a blast and we've decided to spend our summer traveling and working different gigs before starting college in the fall. Will and Maverick are tagging along as our "body guards"—their words, not ours, but in a sense that's what they are. I'm looking forward to going out on the road with my favorite people, doing something I love, and putting the past behind me.

I received a call from someone so unexpected a couple days after the news of Jason Hoover broke asking me to meet her at the local coffee shop. I ordered my drink and took a seat, waiting patiently until five minutes crept to ten. When fifteen minutes hit, I got up and slung bag over my shoulder to head out. I have better things to do than sit around and wait. As I turn to walk away from the table in a huff, I hear, "Please, wait." I slowly turn back to see Ashley hiding behind a pair of sunglasses. Even with sunglasses, it's unmistakable who she is. Her striking, almost white blonde hair is a dead giveaway. She slowly lifts the glasses to rest on her head and takes a seat. I sit down again and wait patiently to hear what she so desperately needs to say. Her gaze drifts down to the table briefly, then she glances back up to me. She's not the same snarky Ashley. She looks sad, like she hasn't been sleeping very well.

"I wanted to know…" she trails off. "When you warned me about Jason, did he do something…" She's unable to speak the word. The word that had taken me so long to admit and say myself. The word I'm no longer ashamed to say. I decide to just tell her. Before, I wouldn't have told her, but considering we now have a sort of emotional connection, she needs to know.

"Ashley, he raped me over a year ago." Looking at her directly, I watch her eyes get big. She doesn't expect this for some reason. I continue, "I didn't tell anyone for a long time and I finally broke; it's not something you can keep hidden forever. I'm doing a lot better, though, and getting help."

"Why didn't you tell me all of this when you warned me?" She snaps.

The 'old' Ashley begins to peek through and my retort is somewhat biting. "Would *you* have told someone who is a constant bitch toward you, *your* most private secret? Would you? Ashley, I tried to warn you, but you can't honestly think I would've told you any details. For God's sake, you thought I was trying to 'steal' him away from you, which couldn't have been further from the truth." I stand up to leave, shocked over her outburst. I don't have to take this shit, and I didn't have to come. I won't let her blame me for someone else's actions.

In true Ashley fashion, she huffs out a breath and looks away. "No, I wouldn't have told me, either." She says resigned.

I sit down for just a moment and softly say, "I'm sorry for what happened to you, Ashley. Nobody deserves that; *ever*. But you can get past this, maybe not forget, but it will get better."

She looks up, a couple small tears visible and quickly wipes them away. "I know you tried to tell me, and I didn't listen." She looks away before adding, "Thanks for trying."

"I would have tried twenty more times to keep what he did to you from happening." She doesn't turn to look or acknowledge me, which says I've been dismissed.

Before leaving I say, "I hope one day you can learn to truly be happy, Ashley." With my parting words, I turn and continue out.

I haven't seen or heard from Ashley since that day, but I meant every word. In a way, it was therapeutic for me. I got to say my piece and close that small chapter; one that otherwise might have always lingered.

I continue my counseling with Dr. Heart, as well as my group sessions. Will has come with me several times to appointments with Dr. Heart. I want to have a healthy relationship, and he's learned more about me than he probably ever wanted. But, he's also been able to, little by little, let go of his guilt from seeing me in that truck and thinking the worst. I've become great friends with several of the girls in group. We found things in common above and beyond the fact we all were raped. I introduced them to Charlie, Maverick and Will and we hung out several times.

For so long, I was ashamed of myself, feeling like a victim. I will never consider myself a victim, ever again. Drinking a glass of alcohol didn't put me in the position to be raped. That was all on Jason Hoover...*not* me.

I've realized the strength in myself and in my family, which naturally includes Will and Maverick. I know myself better, and I know what I'm capable of, and what I can handle. I'm finally been able to stand up in group and proclaim: My name is Tori, and I'm a survivor.

I will never forget what happened to me, but the pain dulls over time. My dreams get less and less, getting pushed deeper in my memory, but this time, it's okay because I tackled it head on, and now I can let go.

I don't know what I would have done without Will and his constant patience with me. When I needed extra strength, he was there to give me some of his. When I felt like crying, his shoulder was there to lean on. When

I needed a hug, his arms where there to wrap around and comfort me. I'm not alone, but it took me going through this entire experience to see that I'm a very blessed girl.

I...
I was strong.
I was brave.
I was in love.
I was loved.
I thought one drink to loosen up.
I thought that was all it was.
I was wrong.

I am not brave.
I am not strong.
I am not in love.
I am not loved.
I have lost my innocence.
I can not go on with my shame!
I will never find anyone that could ever love me past and all.

I will be strong again.
I will be brave again.
I will be in love again.
I will be loved again.
I will make it through.
I will go on with my shame.
I will over come everything.
I will find someone who can love me past and all.

I am strong again.
I am brave again.
I am in love again.
I am loved again.
I have make it through.
I have over come everything.
I have found someone that loves me past and all.

I have survived!!!

Written by Demona, a rape survivor

A Message from Heather

A Note from the Author

Seventeen years ago I went to a party with a girlfriend. We both drank a little too much but I wasn't drunk. I followed a good looking guy into his truck thinking that things wouldn't be taken as far as it was. Unfortunately, I was wrong and NO wasn't something that he understood. I was raped that night and the shame I felt was indescribable. I went home and scrubbed myself clean. I didn't go to the hospital and I didn't immediately go to the police. I kept it from people and for a long time thought that it was my fault. If only I hadn't been drinking then maybe I could've fought him off. Obviously this is preposterous, the guy was a huge football player and no matter how much or little I had drank, I would have never been able to fight myself free.

I could have hit rock bottom but I didn't, I pulled myself back up and chose to get help. Don't get me wrong I made some very foolish mistakes prior to getting help that I thought would make it all go away. It didn't, in fact it made it worse and they are mistakes that I have to live with and think about for the rest of my life. This is my story with a few changes. There are things I've left out for my own privacy, but I've tried to be as forthcoming as possible in my feelings and the numbness that I felt for a very long time. I've had counseling and it has helped in so many ways but I didn't have the guy or the support that Tori has.

We all react differently and there is no right or wrong way. I decided to write my story into Tori's as a way to help me heal. It's still there lingering in my head. Most days I don't think about it but there are those days that my mind lingers back in time. That night will never be forgotten and you don't become miraculously healed but it does get better over time.

There aren't that many books that showcase the healing process of being raped and it was important that I show that. You may ask why I decided to 'come out' and tell everyone that this was my personal story. The reason is simple. I felt that by not being honest, I was showing shame over what had happened to me. You may think this is dumb but this is how I feel. I no longer feel shame and I refuse to feel shame over being raped. For a long time I felt like a victim and it took getting help to realize that I am no one's victim, least of all his. I am a survivor! I survived one of the worst things that has ever happened to me and that, makes me strong as hell!

I never received my closure which is why I chose to give Tori hers. If my story helps someone that has been raped then I've accomplished my goal. Please know that you are not alone but also remember that everyone deals, reacts and heals differently, again there is no right or wrong way.

Below is a list of references for you, should you or someone you know ever need them, (God forbid). The resources available to rape survivors are endless and please know you are never ever alone.

Rape Resource Websites:

http://www.rapeis.org/

http://www.rainn.org/

http://www.rapecrisis.org.uk/resources1.php

http://www.bandbacktogether.com/rape-resources/

http://www.joyfulheartfoundation.org/teenresources_rape.htm

Music Heather listened to while writing Heartstrings

Playlist

Saving Amy - Brantley Gilbert

More than Miles - Brantley Gilbert

Blown Away - Carrie Underwood

Just Give Me a Reason - P!nk & Nate Ruess

Can't Shake You - Gloriana

Easy - Rascal Flats & Natasha Bedingfield

Help Me Remember - Rascal Flats

Tug of War - Carly Rae Jepsen

Get To Me - Lady Antebellum

It Ain't Pretty - Lady Antebellum

Can't Stand the Rain - Lady Antebellum

Golden - Lady Antebellum

Long Teenage Goodbye - Lady Antebellum

All for Love - Lady Antebellum

Little Bit Later On - Luke Bryan

I Want Crazy - Hunter Hays

Sad - Maroon 5

Love Somebody - Maroon 5

Highway Don't Care - Tim McGraw & Taylor Swift

Done - The Band Perry

Don't Let Me Be Lonely - The Band Perry

Better Dig Two - The Band Perry

I Won't Give Up - Jana Kramer

Every Storm (Runs Outa Rain) - Gary Allan

The Last Time - Taylor Swift & Gary Lightbody

If I didn't Have You - Thompson Square

I Can't Outrun You - Thompson Square

Landslide - Fleetwood Mac

Maybe Someday - Lonestar

The Coutdown - Lonestar

Amazing - Josh Kelley

Beautiful Disaster - Jon McLaughlin

Beautiful Soul - Jesse McCartney

Better day - Saving Jane

Naïve - The Kooks

Brave Face - Delta Goodrem

In This Life - Delta Goodrem

Falling Slowly - Glen Hansard & Marketa Irglova

Feel This - Bethany Joy Galeotti

Forgive - Rebecca Lynn Howard

Love - Sugarland

Counting Stars - OneRepublic

Whatever She's Got - David Nail

Let It Rain - David Nail & Sarah Buxton

Lego House - Ed Sheehan

God Gave Me You - Blake Shelton

Coming in 2014

A new chapter in the Love Notes Series

Changing Tunes - Synopsis

Ashley Davis is over her high school 'bitch' label and has decided to reinvent herself. College offers a new beginning, a chance to be different. After being assaulted, she's realized that she needs to change and college is just the place to do it. Nobody knows her and she'd like to keep it that way.

Afraid of falling into the same patterns she decides that having no friends, no life and focusing on school is the way to go. That is, until she meets Zeke Whitman who is completely different from anyone she's ever encountered. He's tall, dark and completely geeky hot in his glasses. He also doesn't seem effected by her looks and ignores her completely.

Ezekiel (Zeke) Whitman is the opposite of Ashley Davis. He's always been driven and focused when it comes to school, but when he's forced to partner with a tall, leggy blonde with a slight attitude, he's thrown for a loop. Ashley confuses him, seeming academically driven in one moment, then flirting the next.

Ashley will realize that sometimes Changing Tunes isn't as easy as it sounds. Sometimes you have to keep a little of the person that you were, in order to become the person who you want to be.

I couldn't have done it without you!

Acknowledgements

This wasn't an easy book to write and there are several individuals who had to talk me off of the ledge, several times. It brought a lot of the past back, which made me dwell and remember everything all over again. There were days that it changed how I dealt with everything in life, including my children. There really aren't enough words to express how wonderful and patient my children are. I wrote this book in five weeks and there were days that I was sad and a bit on the snappy side. I ALWAYS felt horrible afterwards and would sit them down and tell them how sorry I was and that I was writing a story about something that had hurt me a long time ago. Questions were asked of course and I did my best to answer while staying vague. They always forgave me and hugged me after. My children are what make me get up every morning - they breathe life into me. I was meant to be their mom and they were meant to be my babies.

Gabriel, Lucas and Jacob, you will never know how much I love you until you have your own children. Gabriel, your sweet compassion and tender heart makes me smile daily. Watching you help your brothers with their school work or helping them read, makes my heart so happy. You're so patient with them and they look up to you and love you so much. I love our talks together and that because you're older, we can joke and see movies that your brothers can't. We always have fun together.

Lucas, my handsome little man and perfectionist, who always lets me know when he needs momma time. I love that at seven, you still love snuggling with me and holding my hand. You are so smart and one day you'll see how very smart you are. You're so hard on yourself, but I see what you can and will be. You, my love are amazing!

Jacob, my baby, who always ends up in my bed. You are the life of the party and provide the much needed entertainment. You amaze me at what you say and know. You, my little Einstein will do well in Kindergarten: you will blow them away!! Thank you for always telling me how beautiful I am, for telling me fifty times a day that you love me and for your sweet kisses. Thank you for always being affectionate with me, especially sensing when I needed it.

This shout out to kids may seem a bit unorthodox in an acknowledgement, but I think everyone should know how absolute lucky and blessed I am.

Tami Norman, my friend, blog partner, critique partner, confidant and so much more. I absolutely positively love you. Sometimes people are brought into our lives at the right time and girl, you were for me. You provide a life line at times that I don't think you realize. I cannot fathom not having you with me and you not being here through this whole thing. Thank you for constantly telling me to take care of me. Thank you for watching out for me, *always*.

Heather Allen, the best thing that ever happened was the day you contacted me about Indie Girl Con and sharing a table. That was the day that I made such an awesome friend as well as another critique partner. We've grown so close. So close that we talk several times a week and for hours at a time. Thank you for listening to everything going on. Remember, that you are AWESOME and a fabulous writer and I look up to you! I love you to bits!

Katie Mac, thank you for gifting me with some of the very best beta readers a girl could have ever asked for and for being just plain wonderful. Julie Deaton, Lara Feldstein, Danielle Hoover, Debi Barnes, Elle Wilson, Lea Marika & Stephanie Mulford. Thank you so much for your input and help! Mwah!

Emily Sarah Lamphear-Mitchell, I brought you on as a beta because I value your opinion and just plain adore you. Thank you for seeing the changes from book one to book two and for your critiques. Thank you for seeing it the way it was intended!

Julie Deaton, girl you've been through this whole journey with me from the beginning, loving and appreciating this story. There wasn't a day that we didn't chat about it and you didn't care. You know what I mean. I adore the heck out of you and everyone should know how absolutely wonderful you are!! You are absolutely, positively AMAZING and everyone should know that!

Danielle Hoover, you are such a good mom and I see your strength every time we talk. I am proud to call you friend. I love our late night chats and your openness. You are so smart and have so much to offer. You my girl, are just beginning and will do great things! I love you to pieces Danielle, and if you ever need a reminder of how awesome you are, contact me. I'll be there to remind you!

Lara Feldstein, THANK YOU for loving my characters and for messaging me wanting more. I love your ideas and thank you for seeing my vision and where I was going. I'm thrilled beyond that you care about them like I do. You're beautiful Lara, and I'm honored that you've shared and been open with me on our talks. Thank you for trusting me.

Krista Ashe, one of my best buds, thank you for always lending an ear. You always listen and provide insight, never judging. Thank you for taking me as I am and putting up with me and never judging me. I love our dinners and would go crazy without them. You are such an amazing person and I truly love you. I'm blessed to have you as my friend.

Kristy Louise, you may be 'the' Book Addict Mumma, but to me you're my friend. Thank you for being the one of few people that I let in. Thank you for crying right along with me and seeing me. Thank you for everything you do, personal and professional! I always love our chats. If you look back, they're rather crazy at times. I love that!

Melanie Dawn, you didn't think you'd get a shout out did ya? I lurve you and our long ass phone conversations. We could talk all damn day, couldn't we? I'm so glad I've got you in my corner as my friend. Thank you for never judging me. <3

Rae Green, thank you for taking on this editing project last minute. Thank you for appreciating and loving my story and seeing it for what it is. You my girl are great and are going to do great things! Now that we've reconnected, I will be here to see you do all of these great things and will be here to help in any way I can!

Marcia Woodell, thanks for just being you and being a friend. Thank you for checking up on me and constantly making sure that I'm okay. The world needs more people like you in it! Mad love for you!

Randy, Sue & Harley Myers and Christina Sharp, thank you, thank you for being excited for my books and for always supporting me. You will never know how much that means to me.

I made a mistake in my Love Notes acknowledgement that I want to rectify in here. Maverick's parents in Love Notes are based off of two people that meant so much to me when I was a teenager. Steve and Junann Bryant have the marriage that we all strive for, not to mention the relationship with their children that we all wish to have. They were there for me when no one else was and I will always be forever grateful to them. There are parents like Maverick's out there; trust me. I will always love you both!

So many people to thank, just for the plain and simple fact that you've always been there for me to lend an ear whenever I needed it. Sarah Dosher, you rock my socks and I wish you knew how awesome you are! Your writing ability astounds me; true story! L.B Simmons, I want to be you when I grow up, lol. I absolutely & positively adore you! Thank you for never changing and staying the same. I love you for that.

Emily Proffitt Plice with Novel Seduction, I love how excited you get over my books and it makes my heart happy. I think you are just one heck of a person and I enjoy chatting with you. One day I'll meet you in person!

Felicia Lynn, you are going on to do great things. Sit back and enjoy the ride and remember to always surround yourself with people that want to see your dreams fly!

My new friends Whitney Pickens & Erica Sutek, how quickly we became friends that fun night. It's the most fun I've had in a very long time. And you never had to use your 'muscle', see I'm harmless, like a pussy cat!

To the many, many bloggers that have helped spread the word, I will forever be eternally grateful to you all!!

Last but not least to the readers that found value in my characters and found something to relate to. Thank you for loving them and wanting more. It thrills me beyond words. This adventure has been a dream come true and would never have become a reality without you. Mwah!

Author Bio & Stalker Links

About the Author

Heather is a devoted mother of three gorgeous boys. She balances spending as much time with them as possible with writing, updating her Into the Night Reviews book blog and her day job. Her love of animals sees her home in Canton, GA bursting with numerous dogs and ferrets.

Heather campaigns passionately for anti-bullying initiatives and has a strong conviction to reduce peoples suffering at the hands of bullies.

A talented singer, who once dreamed of pursuing a career in that field, she has put that goal aside in exchange for her writing. A self proclaimed geek, whatever spare time she has is spent curled on the couch reading and listening to music.

Facebook: https://www.facebook.com/Author.HeatherGunter

Twitter: https://twitter.com/HeatherGunter5

Blog: http://authorheathergunter.blogspot.com/

Made in the USA
Charleston, SC
30 June 2014